Ships

SUE HOLLISTER BARR

ISBN: 0-9861917-6-0
ISBN-13: 978-0-9861917-6-3

ACKNOWLEDGMENTS

All artwork done by
Josue Ledesma.

"Ships that pass in the night...only a signal shown, and a distant voice in the darkness; So on the ocean of life, we pass and speak ...only a look and a voice, then darkness again and a silence."

Henry Wadsworth Longfellow

A sign read, "Welcome to Kansas."

The only thing Veronica remembered about the place was some *New York Times* article about Kansas being ideal for communicating with extraterrestrial intelligence. Not that its huge radar-dish facility devoted to doing this had ever done so. Anyway, all that mattered to Veronica was hours of land so flat she could just point the Rolls' so-appropriate hood ornament, a winged woman fleeing, at the double yellow line in the middle of the deserted road. Beside her, more distance between her and the ditches at the sides of the road if she started to fall asleep again. Behind her, 90 more miles per hour between her and the very real possibility of a death sentence.

She smirked when she spotted dawn's shimmer in her rearview mirror. *Another glorious day in the second decade of the 21st century?*

Wonder if I'll live long enough to see the 2020s and my 35th birthday. Wonder if anyone will care. The double yellow line disappearing under the middle of the Rolls was beginning to lull her to sleep again.

She squirmed and stretched in the driver's seat till she could smell the leather of its upholstery. Rolling the window all the way down, she all but drowned in the fresh, clean scent of morning. A ray of first light glinted off the highly polished wood of the dash.

Music. Something beautiful enough to keep me awake.

Veronica had thrown her phone and the chauffeur's GPS into the Hudson on her way over the George Washington Bridge, but she didn't think anyone could track the ancient iPod her husband had given her so many summers ago. With a bitter smile she played the message Barrington had recorded on it: "Happy Birthday, Muffin! This is nothing, a tacky trinket. Just wanted to be sure you were the first in the Hamptons to have the latest of its ilk. Your real gift is on the airstrip out back. The price tag on that beauty proves that, yes, I'm another one of those corporate CEOs who would quite literally kill to keep his trophy wife on top of the heap."

At the time, she'd thought the part about

killing was a joke.

Veronica then picked her favorite since early childhood, Ravel's water music. The almost painfully elegant piano in "Menuet Antique" brought a smile. But the soft light of dawn had imbued her new surroundings with a corresponding elegance that didn't hold up under the full, harsh light of day. She shuddered when she first realized that what she'd thought were quaint old farmhouses in the half-light were covered with rusty metal siding. A sign she would have missed in the dark advertised "Girlie Action" at a porn shop.

She checked the gas gauge again. It was going to have to be Kansas. Mile after empty mile flew by. Finally she saw what she was looking for and skidded to a stop, almost hitting the man.

"Wow, lady, I never thought anyone in a Rolls would pick me up!"

Veronica figured her life depended on this hitchhiker's avarice and dishonesty. His quick glance at the maid's purse she'd stolen, that she'd purposely left visible on the seat beside her, gave her hope. "How far are you going?"

She could just imagine the chauffeur's groan as the hitchhiker slid his dusty overalls over the cream-colored piping and onto the mulberry leather upholstery beside her. "Well, it's like this…"

Aside from a Southern twang, the hitchhiker's leisurely start sounded just like her husband talking to his business rivals. This comforted her, since it convinced her that the hitchhiker was about to lie.

"This here town, well, it just don't appreciate me no more. I ain't done nothin' wrong, mind you. They're just…strait-laced." He then spat out the exact words she wanted to hear. "I wanna get as far away from this here shithole as I can."

Veronica thought he was sizing up the maid's uniform she was wearing and hoped he wouldn't spot that her imitation of her maid's red hair was a cheap wig.

After an agonizingly long time, during which she wondered if a less-than-genius IQ would be to her advantage or disadvantage, he finally asked, "What about you? What's a girl like you doin' with a car like this?"

"Can I trust you?"

There was another long silence before he answered in a slow drawl. "Sure…"

Veronica bite her lip; someone once told her that signaled uncertainty. Then she plunged into the script she'd rehearsed all the way across the country: "I worked for Mr.

Hamilton, that CEO guy all over the news. TV says his wife Veronica killed those other CEO guys, but it's not true. Barrington Hamilton just set her up to take the blame for what he did himself. And Veronica Hamilton was too much of a dumb trophy wife to see what her husband was doing."

The hitchhiker fidgeted now, apparently nervous and probably suspicious, then all but emptied a bottle he pulled out of his pocket.

Veronica wanted to scream in fear and frustration. If she couldn't get him to believe her when everything she'd just said—except for pretending to be her own maid—had been the absolute truth, how was she going to get him to believe the pack of lies she was about to tell him? But she could only hope the cheap-smelling alcohol would dull his senses and forge on. "Me? In exchange for hooking up with me, I got the chauffeur to tell Mr. Hamilton this car will be in the shop for a week. I figure I'll be living it up in Vegas by then. I'll never have to work as a maid again."

The hitchhiker hit the bottle again.

Veronica went on with a part she desperately hoped was true. "There are high rollers in Vegas who can pay a whole lot of untraceable cash for a car like this, and they have their own ways of getting things like new license plates."

Silence. Veronica saw in her peripheral vision that he was at least looking the car over, even if only to check for hidden surveillance devices. She pretended to notice a gas station too late to stop for it safely. She had also seen a small country road next to it with a sign announcing it led to a town called Horwedel.

"Oops! Girl's gotta freshen up in the morning!" Veronica screeched into the gas station with a frightening swerve she hoped would convince him he didn't want to ride all the way to Las Vegas with her at the wheel. Laughing as she burnt rubber, she added, "I just love to drive."

When she stopped, she was happy to note it might be awhile before the sleepy proprietor showed up to ask what they wanted.
Veronica looked her passenger up and down, trying to appear attracted to him though it was hard when he responded by grinning, and she noticed how many teeth he was missing.
"Wanna go with me to Vegas? You and me, we can be partners."

"Sure…" The hitchhiker trailed off, a bit drunkenly, she thought and hoped. Then he looked at her funny and bit *his* lip.

Uncertainty? Her heart leaped with the

hope that it was about going with her, not about going to Las Vegas. But, looking into his eyes, she knew she couldn't read eyes. She'd even been diagnosed as having some form of Asperger's syndrome, though she suspected it stemmed from the doctor's desire to make money on its supposed treatment. "I won't take too, too long in the little girls' room. Promise. And I got plenty of money in my purse," she said, patting it and the wallet inside it with the maid's ID. She left it on the seat while exiting the car. "Tell the guy to fill it up if he ever shows up? And pay him with the bigger bills so we'll have change."

Veronica hoped the hitchhiker wouldn't notice the size of the suitcase she slipped out of the back to "freshen up" with before closing the elegant, charcoal-grey door on the car she wanted as far away from her as possible. But she'd hardly closed the rusty door of the lady's room before she heard the Rolls peel out with a swerve twice as frightening as the one she'd come in with.

Betty Ann was smart enough to know that if anyone at the Horwedel Call Center was laughing, it was at her. But she didn't care what any of the twenty people still living in Horwedel thought. She wasn't "paranormal," or whatever that fancy word was that meant she was scared of people when she didn't have to be.

Stupid people. They usually laughed about her boobs being twice as big as the rest of her. Or what she wore to work.

Betty Ann's clothes were real old, especially for someone so young, but she was always careful to match the colors. What did they expect when they didn't even pay minimum wage at that damned call center? At least it was off the books so she could get away with a phony name. That way she could still collect what Social Security paid her because they thought she was too nuts to work.

Betty Ann was also smart enough to know the boss made a mistake when he ignored her warning against having that tech guy from SETI moonlight at the call center. That tech guy had stolen shit from SETI, that place where they searched for "extraterrorists," or whatever the word was for that critter from outer space she now heard in between calls. Very big mistake letting the SETI guy fix the wireless with that shit. Betty Ann had learned enough about extraterrorists from sneaking peeks at the boss' wife's tabloids to know that could only lead to trouble. Very big bad trouble.

"Horwedel City Limit."

Veronica looked past the sign. "*City*"? All she could see was a few trailers up ahead. And she was now so tired she couldn't stop tripping in the dust.

At least, on her way down the road from the gas station, she'd scuffed up the Stuart Weitzman $50,000 Nikes Barrington had bought her long ago. She hoped no one would notice that the dust-encrusted sparkles edging the Nike logos were actually eleven carats of chocolate-colored diamonds.

And her new wig was much more comfortable, of far better quality than the cheap one she'd worn first to mimic her maid's red hair. Veronica had been quite happy to leave it, and the maid's uniform, in the gas station's dumpster. She just hoped all that short dark hair now brushed forward into her face, along with the heavy eye makeup she never wore, would be enough to keep anyone from recognizing her facial features. It was a lot harder to see past than her own long blonde hair, which she wore back.

That reminded her of her picture in the passport she'd left purposely visible in a garbage can at JFK. Since she'd cleared final boarding before miraculously switching places with that disappointed standby, would her dear husband Barrington believe she'd flown to Paris and entered France with a phony passport? If only she'd had more time to plan. Especially since she'd stupidly forgotten to ditch her phone at the airport along with her purse and passport. Halfway across the George Washington Bridge she'd remembered and heaved her phone out the window hard, praying that it hit the water.

Veronica tripped again. It twisted her ankle, but she almost laughed when she saw that one of the diamonds in the shoes Barrington had thought so much of had all but fallen off in the dust of "fly-over" America.

Barrington…

She staggered to her feet and kept walking.

Her husband…

One minute she was laughing with Barrington over what she'd assumed was only paparazzi sensationalism about him implicating her in the CEO killings—if those murders had even actually taken place. The next minute, he was laughing at her and telling her she should try and find her own personal legal counsel. But she knew Barrington's lawyers and other even-less-scrupulous associates, who included anyone in power in the district attorney's office and the police department. Collectively, they could have gotten Abraham Lincoln convicted for his own assassination.

Not far past the Horwedel City Limit sign, Veronica fell to one knee, got up, and then couldn't stop herself from falling onto the other knee. Dust choked her. One question, like a mirage, flickered in and out of her consciousness: Why did Barrington tip her off?

She forced herself back to her feet. As she dragged her frazzled self onward, other questions preyed on her: Would the hitchhiker take the Rolls far away, or just get so drunk he totaled it ten miles from her present location? Was he smart enough to unload it in Las Vegas in a way that would delay, if not prevent, its discovery? If not, was he dumb enough to forget exactly where he left "the maid"?

Would the real maid, spooked by the publicity over the murders and fleeing, ever resurface? How long before the chauffeur, whose absence due to a family emergency had made it possible for Veronica to take one of their Rolls Royces, return to discover a car was missing?

"Room for Rent."

It was only a yellowed piece of paper taped to a trailer's door, but Veronica stumbled up the rickety steps and rang the doorbell. She rifled through the cheap purse she'd bought at JFK: only two hundred dollars left. *Damn the thousand-dollar-a-day ATM cash withdrawal limit!* And the hideous mileage the Rolls had gotten for the last thousand-plus miles. And the sure knowledge that using a credit card or pawning jewelry would be tantamount to leaving a trail of bread crumbs.

Her obsessive concentration finally cracked. Her focus blurred. Purse she bought at JFK? She remembered her childhood fascination with that long-dead president and the only gift her father ever gave her: a chance to read a rare, unpublished manuscript of JFK's.

"Ya want the room?" Dressed in something that even the person who scrubbed

Veronica's toilets wouldn't touch, the woman standing in the trailer's open doorway sounded ecstatic. Of course Veronica couldn't read eyes. But she could see these eyes were elderly and squinting through glasses so thick she didn't think the woman would ever be able to describe her accurately. *Perfect!*

"How much?"

"It's a real nice room. Bed's all made up and everything. I can't let it go for less than a hundred."

Two nights! Veronica only had enough for two—

"And that'll be due and payable right now, missy, and promptly on the first of every month."

Month? "Yes, ma'am." She dove into her purse and shoved a hundred at the woman.

"Now I don't cotton to sharing my kitchen with no one. You do got a hot plate in your room, and you can use the left crisper drawer in the fridge. My name's Margret. Here's your key."

"Where's the room?"

"Come on in."

There was no light inside the trailer, and Margret didn't turn one on. Stacks of boxes all but covered the few windows. Veronica

13

hoped it was because Margret's vision was so bad that even light wouldn't help.

She didn't even care when she stubbed her toe in the dark. She just barely remembered yanking her suitcase into what she thought was a dark closet in the back and falling onto a tiny bed. Just before she lost consciousness she heard Margret mutter something about getting her name later.

Veronica woke up refreshed. With her eyes adjusted to the dark, she saw moonlight struggling to get around a curtain that fluttered over her window, so she pushed the curtain aside. Pearly light poured over her. Outside was the most magnificent night sky she had ever seen. Vast. Quiet.

She reached into her suitcase for one of the very few luxuries she'd brought, a dog-eared postcard from before she married Barrington. It was from a boy she'd met in Paris with hair as dark as the wig she wore now. In the moonlight she traced the one word he'd written on it, his last name: Charbonneau.

Fitting. They had walked through the

Louvre together, hardly speaking a word.
When they saw something so beautiful they
thought their hearts would break, they silently
kissed the tears from each other's eyes.
Endlessly making love in his moonlit attic,
they were above cheap, vacuous prattle.
Veronica tilted her head back in the
moonlight now. The memory of M.
Charbonneau inside her was so exquisite it
brought tears.

  She turned the postcard over. He'd sent
her an ancient sepia photograph by Eugene
Atget, a Parisian who shared their disdain for
chatter. M. Atget photographed just after
dawn, catching the misty promise of infinity
in each new day before any people showed up
to sully his shots. This was a garden shot
from Versailles: Glowing horizon. Lush
vegetation in the background. Classical
statuary in the foreground. Silent and serene.

  Veronica leaned over to close the window
so she could decorate it by propping the
postcard up against it. Then she lay back
down in bed and smiled at the postcard
bathed in moonlight on her windowsill till her
eyes closed again.

When Veronica stirred next, in the wee hours, she felt like she'd been bitten by a hundred mosquitoes. That seemed odd since the window was shut. Then she thought she saw small, round bugs in bed with her, of a type she'd never seen before, but figured it was just a dream.

She awoke in the full light of day to a torso covered with angry bites and the sight of a giant cockroach pausing on her beloved postcard to clean its antennae. Behind it, through the window where she'd seen the magnificent night sky, she now saw a rusty refrigerator in a weed-choked yard littered with garbage. Inside the trailer a TV blasted canned laughter as painfully stupid sitcom lines grated on her last nerve.

Veronica leapt to her feet and snatched her postcard from the cockroach. She was going to stuff it and the clothing she must have pulled off in her sleep back into her suitcase, demand her hundred back, and flee. But the sitcom was replaced by a tabloid-esque facsimile of news: "Our exclusive sources are wondering if Barrington Hamilton's wife ever boarded that flight to Paris."

Veronica froze, then threw her

possessions back on the bed. Leave this hundred-dollar-a-month hideout in the middle of nowhere? With only a hundred left? Who was she kidding? She blinked back tears, clawed at her bites, and flew into a fury of frustration trying to kill the cockroach. But it easily sidestepped her every effort, still intent on getting what was apparently a particularly troublesome speck of dirt off its antenna. Emotionally spent at last, Veronica drew herself up and rewarded her more-than-worthy adversary with a smart salute. "You're certainly big enough," she said to the cockroach, "so you must be Toto. Would…that we were not in Kansas anymore."

A voice from behind her door called, "You finally up?" She might not be able to see, but she could hear.

"Yes, Margret."

"You best be hurrying over to the Horwedel Call Center and get yourself a job or you'll never make next month's rent. But you gotta ditch that nose-in-the-air voice and sound sexy or men'll never pay to get their rocks off with you."

Jason Spirit-That-Soars took another pull of his beloved "firewater" and contemplated, not for the first time, the only other "injun" in Horwedel still standing, the one covered with graffiti in front of the general store. Considerable debate had failed to decide which of the two of them was more wooden since Jason, stereotypes be damned, could hold his liquor.

"Jason, who's got bigger tits, that scrawny little Betty Ann or your boss man's wife, Miss 300-Pounds?" It was Eddie, the consummate retro redneck, who had tormented Jason all his life. Now he was trying to set him up. If he answered, he was being disrespectful to a white woman; if he didn't answer, he was being disrespectful to a white man.

"Oh, Eddie, you know Jason ain't answerin.'" That was Eddie's sidekick, Ike, busy drooling over girlie magazines. Unemployed and always on the streets, they'd followed Jason to the abandoned gas station where he had hoped, in a town with less than twenty people left, he could spend his lunch hour alone. "Besides," Ike added, "can hardly tell what kinda tits that crazy bitch Betty Ann got under them rags she wears."

But, even with his peripheral vision, Jason

could tell that Eddie was intent on his prey and gearing up for his next attack. "Hey, Ike, ain't that big old nasty scar on the back of the injun's neck where we decked him one with that trash can when we was in the second grade? Sure was funny."

Jason took a huge slug of firewater, pocketed his flask, and gathered the drawings of the prairie he'd been working on. He kept his face as expressionless as the graffiti-covered wooden Indian's. When he was sure of himself he rose to his feet to return to work.

Shareholders countrywide who'd failed to mail in their proxy votes were awaiting his call, Jason told himself with the same bitter humor that prompted him to use words like "firewater" and "injun." He almost cracked a smile at his own sarcasm, but remembered his pledge of brotherhood to The Great Graffitied One. What was important was that Jason's favorite paleface—who, stereotypes be damned, couldn't hold his liquor—awaited Jason's flask. Ironically the town wino, who worked with Jason and was waiting for him at the call center, was the only one left with the clarity to call things as they really were.

As Jason walked back to the call center, he gazed sideways across the open prairie that was visible between the tattered remnants of the town. Then he heard Ike's sharp whistle, the one usually reserved for Playboy centerfolds, and looked back toward the call center. Even dressed, and modestly at that, the strange woman with the short dark hair who was walking towards the call center ahead of Jason was a knock-out.

Its sign read, "Horwedel Call Center."

Veronica was approaching what must have been a storefront in the 1930s. Now its front windows were covered with rusty sheet metal except the two windows in the middle that angled in toward the recessed entrance. Those were so grimy she couldn't see what was inside. But she kept trudging through the dust till she'd walked through the call center's front door.

She was greeted by the stench of stale urine and the sound of a toilet running. A telltale puddle gave away its location behind a flimsy wall that was broken near the bottom.

"Name?" The woman asking weighed 250, if not 300 pounds. What she took to be the woman's reception desk was a dilapidated card table piled high with bags of Cheese Doodles and other junk food. But behind her was a crude sign saying they only paid their workers in cash, no checks. For Veronica, unable to use a bank account with her name, that meant everything.

Still, the table was littered with empty Beano containers that, from what she could smell even over the urine, had done little to alleviate the woman's problem with gas.

Even when trying to evade the electric chair, some alternatives could be daunting, and Veronica was momentarily caught off-guard. "Veron—*Vera!*" She caught herself, then managed a wry smile as she also lied about her last name, "Charbonneau."

The woman was writing, her flyaway hair fluttering about. "That's Vera S-H-A-R-E-B-E-A-N-O, right?"

"Uh… Yes, that's fine."

"What kinda name is that?"

"French."

"Well, la de da. You can sit over there till my hubby gets to you, Miss…" She paused, then laughed. "Miss Share Beano." She laughed some more and smiled broadly, revealing a wad of purple gum she then smacked. Its fake-grape aroma managed to be even more nauseating than everything else

Veronica could smell.

From where she perched on a folding chair, Veronica could see into the dark cavern of the call center.

A teeny woman with a huge chest was dressed in rags, though impeccably color-coordinated. In her early twenties, she was on the phone, describing a blow job in terms that managed to make an act Veronica enjoyed sound utterly repugnant.

A Native American man slid into his seat in the next cubicle. He was soon on the phone, asking a shareholder of an absurdly insignificant mutual fund if she would like to vote her shares according to the recommendation of its board.

In the cubicle across from him, an obviously inebriated wino, peddling magazine subscriptions on the phone, stood to take a flask from the Native man. Spotting Veronica, the wino did a vaudevillian double-take that would have done W.C. Fields proud. Unable to read his eyes, she had no idea what that meant.

She also thought she overheard someone taking an order for plus-sized clothes but couldn't see the speaker.

"Vera?" Just the way it was said constituted rape. The obese woman's greasy-haired "hubby" followed up with a hand on Veronica's arm that managed to grope the side of her breast. "Betty Ann's script is hot, ain't it? Here, read it. See if you can make a blow job sound as good as she does. I'll just stroke your arms to get you in the mood."

She took the paper he offered and did try. But the description of snorting whatever cum she couldn't cram up her butt stopped her cold.

"That's all you got?" her prospective boss snapped, raking thick fingers through his greasy hair. "You sound like friggin' royalty, Miss Share Beano. I can't use you on incoming 900. I got no use for you at all, unless…" There was no mistaking his assault on her breasts then.

Veronica sprang to her feet, remembering all too painfully that Margret had said this was the only work within walking distance. And the cash payment. "I need this job *very badly,* but…"

In the moment of standoff silence that followed, the Native American could be heard struggling with a shareholder. "Ma'am, I'm not quite sure why the Initial Public Offering makes a new investment advisor agreement with the fund necessary. May I put you on hold while I check with my boss?" He hit a button on his phone console and looked at the obese woman's husband.

"Jason…how the fuck should I know?" was the boss' response.

"The Investment Company Act of 1940 renders all previous agreements null and void," said Veronica, "if there's a change of ownership as a result of the IPO. The fund is making provisions for a replacement agreement."

Jason got back on the phone with the shareholder and explained the 1940 Act.

The boss yelled at his wife. "Miss 300, we got enough proxy solicitation for another phone rep, or have you let Pakistan steal all our fucking business?"

Young Betty Ann leapt to her feet. She was so skinny it looked like her huge chest might topple her over. "He's coming," she announced. Then she fought the wino for Jason's flask and won.

"Who's coming, Betty Ann?" asked the disgruntled wino. "Your client, in which case a trip to Lourdes is in order to celebrate the miracle? Maybe Jesus Christ, in which case this would only be the second time. Or no, who is it you're always saying is coming? If not JFK's assassin's family that's been trying to shut your family up for generations, it must be one of your 'extraterrorists.'"

Histus preferred to think of the one "sense" he had left as "smell," though sensing the chemical content of anything near the ship hardly qualified. There was nothing pleasurable about it, nothing delectable about detecting the H_2O needed to fuel the ship he'd been forced to become a part of. Even perceiving something that would have titillated him when he had a body—rather than something toxic like H_2O—gave him no real joy and did precious little to relieve the incomprehensible tedium of deep-space travel.

But like any other senses—his long-gone sense of remote texture or of weight differentiation—sensing anything at all divided one moment from the next. There was the moment when he "smelled" an usual amount of stellar gas passing on the starboard side and the moment when he "smelled" that same unusual amount switch to their port side. This gave him the only thing he cared about now: a sense of time passing, at least infinitesimal progress toward the moment

when they would arrive at their destination.
Then those lucky enough to have uploaded
themselves into parts of the ship the last time
their enemies attacked—now the only ones
left of his species—would find a way to grow
new bodies. Somehow.

"My name is Vera Charbonneau, and I'm
calling on a recorded line about your
investment in—"

Click. Another shareholder hung up on
her. Veronica regretted not getting the proxy
vote to make the boss happy, certainly
preferable to making him happy in any other
way. But truthfully she yearned for the quiet
in between the outgoing calls fed to her by the
automatic dialer. There was something in that
silence that wasn't quite silent. She'd noticed
it the first time she put on the earphones.
Something infinite like the night sky she'd
seen from her trailer window.

Teeny Betty Ann could be heard
describing a sexual activity Veronica didn't
even think was possible. Jason was answering
so many questions that she figured his
shareholder would soon ask what each of the

board's trustees was having for dinner. But Veronica concentrated on that odd emptiness, which wasn't quite empty, between calls. She gazed longingly into the postcard she'd propped up in her cubicle. If she concentrated, she could tune out the voices around her. She could imagine that she, and perhaps the cockroach she'd named Toto, weren't in Kansas anymore. They, along with whatever she sensed coming through her earphones in the quiet, were with photographer Eugene Atget in the gardens of Versailles.

Betty Ann might be young, but she wasn't stupid. She knew that the injun's friend, that damn wino pushing magazine subscriptions, thought she was. But she knew better. After all, how many people still alive knew about the little kid on the grassy knoll who had really killed JFK? Four. The killer, his daughter and her husband, and Betty Ann. That's how many.

What the wino said about Jesus Christ? Disrespectful. To Jesus and to her. Damn wino thought she was stupid enough to believe that Jesus Christ's second coming was happening now.

And she wasn't stupid when it came to that new girl, neither. Betty Ann knew who she really was.

The customer she was talking to finished with a squeal like a Ginny pig, or whatever those little rat-like things were, instead of the usual satisfied moan. Click.

"You're welcome," Betty Ann said in response to the thank you she so much deserved but hadn't gotten. But then came that noisy time between calls. She started to get scared again. She could hear him; he was getting closer, fast.

At least that injun Jason, surrounded by all his dumb drawings of the prairie, was finally quiet. Jason had his flask back, too, and was too busy checking out the new girl to notice when Betty Ann snatched his flask with shaking hands before his friend the wino got it. Betty Ann wanted to rip them headphones off so she couldn't hear what was in between calls. She was so thankful when the buzz in her ear announced the next caller.

Veronica was starving by break time, but knew she shouldn't spend much. She hurried through the dusty street to the general store. Still, she had time to be offended by the wooden Indian next to the entrance and its graffiti insulting Native Americans. It was even worse than the boss—and everyone else, including herself, since it was the only name she'd heard—calling the woman he'd married by a name that indicated her weight.

"Just look at those, Eddie!" called out one of the two guys always on the street. "New girl's got bigger titties than Miss 300!"

The other guy, Eddie, followed up with a loud whistle.

Veronica calmed when she stepped inside. The store was cool and quiet and smelled of the worn wooden countertops where she found an inexpensive apple. She also bought a cheap little pot and a box of white rice to take home to her hot plate. After grabbing her change from the proprietor's crinkled old fingers, she hurried back to the call center for fear of being late.

Miss 300 held up a cheese-doodle-stained hand as Veronica started to pass her reception desk. "I have something to show you," she said officiously, her uncontrollable hair floating about her like a cloud. She bent over, all but impossible, and extracted something covered in plastic from under her card table. After wiping her hands on her shirt, she removed the plastic.

Veronica's eyes widened. *The wedding album, before firing me? She must have seen her husband assault my breasts.*

With utmost reverence, Miss 300 pulled out a fanzine and pointed to a picture of a gorgeous female star who couldn't have looked more different from what Miss 300 could ever have looked like. "I'll bet even you haven't read the real story about this little piece of work. But I know everything."

Behind Miss 300 the wino rolled his eyes. "If you know everything, why don't you tell her what the boss and Betty Ann are doing right now?"

Miss 300 gnashed her teeth but didn't answer.

Jason could hardly take his eyes off her no matter how many pulls he took of the "firewater." Even looking away he caught a hint of the general store's fragrant cottonwood in the alluring scent of her skin as she walked by, the sweetness of an apple still on her breath.

The forbidden fruit. At least in this town that time forgot. Or was it his prejudice, not theirs?

Jason might have turned out quite literally like the apple this white bitch had just devoured—part red, part white—but his uncle gave his life rather than let a white man rape Jason's mother.

Double, triple pull on the firewater. Maybe if... He pushed aside his other drawings and got out a new piece of paper. He started with the dark, short hair—though that was the part of her that seemed the least...her.

Veronica ate as much plain rice as she could stand and waited in Margret's trailer for the garish light of day to subside. While waiting, she filled the empty margarine containers around the legs of her bed with water. She didn't quite understand why, but she'd noticed the old woman's bed in the living room had these too. She'd seen Margret feeling around them so she could fill them with water, despite her poor eyesight.

Otherwise Veronica avoided looking too closely at her surroundings before sunset.

Finally a shaft of salmon light softened the glare off the gold chevrons in her peeling wallpaper. She felt something wonderful and realized it was her own smile. Diving into her suitcase, she removed another of the few luxuries she'd allowed herself.

She bathed the scrapbook she'd made as a child in the first rays of sunset. For a moment her smile faltered and she shuddered, remembering the sound of her parents' constant, shrill arguments.

But she quickly turned the pages. Like Atget's photographs, there were no people to disturb the beauty of the images she'd collected, touting the treasures and architecture of the 19th century. She remembered only the blessing of having grown up in a 19th-century mansion so huge she could avoid all contact with other people. Like Alice escaping down the rabbit hole, she'd run through endless hallways of empty rooms until she could no longer hear her parents or any of the squabbling servants.

Her playmates were all safe, coming to life from the toile wallpaper or the heavy oil paintings lining the long halls. So what if the same two children, leaping from the endlessly repeating pastoral scenes of the wallpaper, were all two-toned, wine red and ecru? And one could forgive the blotchy, brush-stroked skin of those from the paintings, since they all smiled as they scurried down the halls with her.

Her imaginary playmates never argued. Whenever Veronica asked her mother why she had only one child, her mother told her that her brothers and sisters would have argued constantly.

Histus stopped himself, yet again, from dwelling on the past. But not without remembering that the sense he missed most, unlike the others of his kind uploaded into different parts of the ship, was vibration. He hadn't thought it possible, but he was starting to forget the rhythm of "Eclipse Beats," his favorite musical composition.

Still he had to stop. Almost all that remained of his species had by now driven themselves insane by dwelling on the past. Some of them were uploaded into important parts of an already severely disabled ship that could no longer be accessed, due to their insanity.

He had made fun of the others' gallows humor when they started referring to each other as "it." But he could appreciate their attempt to move beyond the past, and that it was absurd to keep thinking of himself as male.

He just couldn't let go of what it meant to be male, his adoring offspring beneath his wing, stowed securely in a pouch that females just didn't have. Or what it felt like to fly under a female and bring those young into being. While other memories dimmed, there was no dimming the memory of that particular vibration.

Jason could feel the last strands of sunset tickle his face like his ancient Tali's old feather duster. As soon as it was fully dark, cooler air swirled around him as if a wave had finally broken over his head. He started walking back home across the field. Running his fingers through the vegetation, he smirked at the old Native American cliché of smelling each plant he passed, until he suddenly caught the scent of something else.

Vera.

He turned in the direction of her fragrance and saw the telltale indentation amidst stalks of corn. Her hair was visible, blowing in unison with the tassels atop the stalks. He didn't have his flask with him, or his drawing materials, to redirect his attention from her.

Veronica marveled over the baby corn she could barely make out in the starlight. Never finding her way back to Margret's blaring TV wouldn't be a complete tragedy.

Breathing deeply, she drank in the night air, far sweeter than the expensive liqueurs Barrington had tried to woo her with when they first met. She almost smiled, remembering his feverish efforts, his nervously twisting his little-finger ring around: a priceless 9th-century Anglo-Saxon heirloom with his ancestor Cynefrid's name on the band. But she also remembered her mother yelling every time Veronica complained about his lack of depth. Or insisted she'd rather starve than marry for money. Her mother screeched about their family's reversals of fortune and what her daughter owed them. She could still hear her mother's oft-repeated summation, "Besides, you're far too gently bred to live in a trailer." Funny.

Something important tickled the back of her mind. Was it about her mother? No, it was something about why Barrington had tipped her off about seeking legal counsel. She pounced on it, as if trying to remember a dream, but it wiggled free of her grasp yet again.

There was hardly a sound, the gentlest rustling. Veronica flinched, realizing she wasn't alone. The first thing she saw was Jason's hair silhouetted by the stars. She smiled, remembering that it was every bit as dark as M. Charbonneau's. But then she noticed something odd above him, in the constellation Orion. Where there should have been only three stars in Orion's belt there were now four.

"Vera."

There was something wrong with Jason's voice. An intensity. Veronica didn't know what else to say, so she held up a baby corn. "Have you seen these?"

Too quickly his hand brushed against hers as he examined what she was showing him.

His hand was sweaty, and he was breathing a bit heavily.

She stepped back, trying to figure out what was wrong. "Been…drinking?"

"Wish I had!"

The stars glittered overhead. Veronica thought she knew the way back to Margret's trailer. "Walk with me?"

"Sure."

"Know the constellations?"

"By heart." His voice had deepened.

"See Orion?"

"Yeah," he said, but he was still looking at her.

"Isn't there an extra star in his belt?"

He stopped, looking up. "Shit, you're right!"

They stood together, swaying in unison before an urgent wind.

Finally Veronica got them walking toward Margret's again. "It wasn't there last night."

He was looking at her again. "You come out here every night too?"

A prickle of caution prompted her clumsy evasion. "Lived here all your life?"

"All my life and all the lives of a hundred generations before me."

"Town like this, how do they treat you?"

"The only good injun is…at least wooden.

That's why I drink."

"Then why do you stay?"

"I won't leave this land. Or abandon the bones of those hundred generations. I know it's a fucking cliché, but can you smell it in the stillness of the night? The wealth of their memories blanketing the earth? The hushed reverence?"

Veronica remembered the hushed reverence she'd felt in the stillness of the abandoned wings of the house she grew up in. The feeling that her ancestors in the paintings, long dead, detested the irreverent racket of her parents and the servants as much as she did. "Yes," she said slowly, just as they arrived within earshot of Margret's TV, which broke the spell. "But we both better get some sleep, or the shareholders will have us for breakfast tomorrow. Good night."

Betty Ann was smart enough to know she had to give the boss head to keep her job, especially now that his wife knew. But she was still scared of being on the outs with his wife, and, besides, she almost felt sorry for Miss 300. What a wallow, or whatever those

super-fat seals were called! Even her hair
floated around as far away from her as
possible, as if it were trying to escape. Even
the friggin' mobile Miss 300 was making out
of a rusty coat hanger looked like it wanted to
get away.

Maybe Betty Ann could smooth things
over between them by boosting Miss 300's
ego and giving her life some of that celebrity
glam she loved so much. Betty Ann cleared
her throat and tried her damnedest to sound
sincere. "You know everything."

Miss 300 glared at her.

Betty Ann gulped. Maybe that wasn't the
best thing to say after all. "I mean about
important people, like celebs."

"And?"

"You're real smart. I bet you even know
who the new girl is."

"Of course I do!" Miss 300 snapped, then
paused. "Who do *you* think she is?"

"Well I'm not as good as you are, but I
was kind of thinking she might be, you know,
that missing actress whose husband was
cheating on her?"

"Obviously!" Miss 300 bellowed before
wrinkling her brow in thought. Finally she
beamed, then actually smiled at Betty Ann.

Of course Betty Ann knew better. She

was smart enough to know the real truth of who that new girl was.

When Veronica fell into step far behind Jason on the way to work, it spooked her at first that he reacted immediately, half-turning back towards her. Then the sun sparkled on his magnificently sculpted cheekbones and skin rich with the color of copper.

She saw a hesitation, as if he struggled with some indecision, before he turned away and settled into an easy forward pace again.

Veronica found herself hypnotized by his effortless stride, then chided herself as she recognized her parents' attitude within her. Jaded socialite lured by the "noble savage"? Gliding silently through the forest, perhaps? How very upper-crust WASP of her to be attracted to the exotic.

And in this awful place where she'd been forced to hide to save her life? As if on cue, Eddie's constant sidekick—the one who was always leering at girlie magazines and, along with Eddie, apparently unemployed and always on the streets—whistled at her again.

But then she returned her attention to

Jason, remembering the majesty of the night sky in Kansas and his hushed reverence for the past that she felt as strongly as he did. Despite her problems reading other people, she imagined she could see as much depth in Jason's dark eyes as she could in a night sky.

Was it only because she was at last free of Barrington? She compared Jason's walk to Barrington's, which was jarring, staccato and thoughtless. It was as if Barrington assumed it was up to the ground to accommodate him with a perfectly level surface, rather than up to him to adjust to the ground.

As Jason disappeared into the call center ahead of her it occurred to her that, except for the other's alabaster skin, Jason looked a lot like M. Charbonneau.

Inside, Miss 300 stood in front of Veronica's desk, and Jason's friend, the wino who didn't seem to ever leave the call center where he worked, was fighting a losing battle to suppress his laughter.

"Ta da," said Miss 300, stepping aside.

A mobile made of empty Beano containers now hung over Veronica's desk.

"Get it, Miss Share Beano?" Miss 300 got close to her while walking past. "I really hope you like it." She was now so close no one else could hear her. "Even though you and I both know that isn't your real name."

Veronica staggered back from her.

Miss 300 went on. "I know everything about people like you. But people like you and me have to stick together. I know your story, but it'll be okay." She patted her, leaving a layer of cheese-doodle dust on her shoulder, and was gone.

Veronica's phone box was blinking; the boss must have turned her automatic dialer on before she'd even sat down. Before she had the earphones over her ears she said "Hello?" into the mic.

"…for the fact that a top CEO, despite his current legal problems, recommended this rinky-dink fund I'd never put up with—"

"Hello, my name is Vera Charbonneau and I'm calling on a recorded line. May I speak to…to…" She was fumbling with her computer's log-on. She had to use the mouse because the tab key wouldn't work. After several unsuccessful password attempts she finally realized the tab key hadn't worked because she'd hit Caps Lock instead. "To…"

"The Queen of Sheba? Lawrence of Arabia, perhaps?"

The name finally appeared on her screen. "Antoine Dubois?"

"Well at least you can pronounce French.

As a matter of fact you have quite the voice for someone in your position. Anyway, I'm sure you're calling, yet again, to get my proxy vote. I've even labeled your number on my caller ID as 'Painfully Persistent Proxy People' and, yet again, I will not vote for anything over the phone."

Veronica was hardly listening. How had Miss 300 known? How far was the next supposedly in-the-middle-of-nowhere-where-no-one-knows-anything town? Did she have enough money for a bus at least part of the way? Would Margret give her back any of her $100? Did she dare draw attention to her departure by asking for the money she'd earned so far at the call center?

She had been strong for so long. All so she could spend her days listening to skinny Betty Ann describe blow jobs and her nights sleeping in a closet to the tune of Margret's TV. What would she have to do in the next town?

"So if I said I wasn't going to vote over the phone yesterday, I'm not going to vote over the phone today or tomorrow. Do not call again." Click.

"Hello? Hello? Who's calling?"

No space between calls this day.

"Hello, my name is Vera Charbonneau

and I'm calling…"

On his way home from work Jason knew, for the second time that day, that she was behind him. What he couldn't understand this time was her hurried approach. He almost jumped out of his skin when she grabbed his bare arm.

"Do you have…or do you know anyone who has…a computer with internet access I can use?"

She was still clinging to his arm, so Jason flipped his flask out of his back pocket for a long pull. "I've got one."

She dropped his arm suddenly, as if catching herself doing something distasteful.

Ouch. But Jason upended the flask instead of pointing out that, unlike red wine, red skin didn't stain. "Did you want to use it now?"

"Yes. Please."

They walked together. He noted that the dust caressed her ankles. Even the breeze took liberties, ruffling her clothes. Eddie and Ike, coming out of the general store to end one of the rare moments when they couldn't be found on the street, froze in horror at the sight of Vera and Jason together. They'd just love it when they saw him take her into his trailer. Jason's muscles tensed before he remembered his Pledge of Woodenness to The Great Graffitied One. The foolish paleface at his side was going on about how she found a wooden Indian offensive.

"Histum?"

"Hist*us*," he sent back, persisting in retaining the masculine form of his name. But he was happy to honor her desire to be neutered by addressing her as Shishum, since the Shisha he remembered was a pathetic irritant when she had a body. Couldn't fly a wing stroke without knocking into someone.

"I'm getting transmissions," Shishum sent. "Old and current. Two planets in the solar system we just entered."

"Is the current a threat?"

"Only to themselves."

"Still no imagery?"

"Still no workaround for the software's assumption that I've still got a body to interpret it with."

"Did you hail the current?" Histus asked,

hoping the current was advanced enough to repair the ship, if not its uploaded passengers.

"I initiated with one of our standard baseline intelligence tests, the ability to determine that something is a musical composition. Sent your favorite, 'Eclipse Beats.' It'll take them a while to get it, but I did set you up with a direct communications link in case they answer. Any luck locating our next source of liquid H_2O?"

"With what little tech we've got left, your range is pathetic, but my range for sensing chemical content is even worse. I won't be able to positively confirm H_2O till we're right on top of it."

"Our enemies did well for themselves by destroying all our long-range sensors," Shishum sent. "Can we even be sure that this galaxy is the one with our new home at its core?"

"That much is certain," Histus sent, hoping he was right.

"What happens if we run out of liquid H_2O?"

"Without fuel we drift, but we'll run into some kind of H_2O that we should be able to convert eventually, even as crippled and severely damaged as we are. There's plenty of it around." He didn't think it necessary to discuss how long "eventually" could be with no active propulsion system.

"And, once we reach our new home—in a gas giant at the center of *this* galaxy, right?—we can figure out a way to grow new bodies? Reassure me on this again. Are you absolutely positive?"

"Yes," he lied, then added to his send: "What about the old transmissions from the second planet? Any useful information about local resources there?"

"No," Shishum sent back. "Too old."

"Usual migratory pattern? The old being farther from the star than the current?"

"Yes. Fourth and third from the star."

While Jason went into a back room to get his laptop, Veronica took a moment from obsessing over her situation to look in wonder at her surroundings. Unlike Margret's trailer, Jason's was immaculate. But it was more than that.

Computer-generated art, printed on thick brown paper, covered the walls. Most were collages in which images of Native American and Asian antiquities were combined and reshaped. Their sense and symmetry were striking.

But when Veronica stood to enjoy them more, each changed like an optical illusion. One became a picture of an old woman, in different poses depending on her viewing angle. Another became the open prairie she'd glimpsed beyond the confines of the town. In a third she finally recognized the face of the wooden Indian from the general store. But when she stood in a different place the wooden Indian's face was replaced by Jason's.

Turning away from these paper miracles, she found an elaborate pagoda constructed of Lego blocks. She smiled, delighted by the details. Beside it was an open book describing how two Native Americans were shipwrecked on the shores of Holland around 60 B.C.

"Here," Jason said, handing her a laptop.

"Thanks. Don't let me get in your way. I'll be out of here soon." She felt awkward, as if she'd been caught stealing his treasures.

"No rush."

Veronica flipped open the laptop. Without Jason's creations to enchant her, reality hit like a fist. Google. Barrington Hamilton.

The first and third links were already purpled, clicked into before. *Damn!* Stupidly, she cringed visibly when she looked up at Jason.

He had seated himself as far away from her as possible. But he was looking from Veronica to the drawing paper he held, making broad strokes with a charcoal pencil between huge guzzles from a bottle of whiskey. Of course asking him if he'd ID'd her would be as stupid as assuming a private browser window could escape detection from anyone with enough computer savvy to have generated his artwork.

All she could do was confine herself to clicking into the same two links Jason already had. His having done so first would cover her own tracks to a degree.

The good news was that the hitchhiker had at least made it to Las Vegas before foolishly trying to sell the Rolls to a car museum. When asked how he got the car, his description of Veronica dressed up like the maid had matched the real maid—who was still missing. An unexpected bonus was that he claimed the maid had "given" him the Rolls—apparently due to his prowess in bed—in Colorado, not Kansas. That would put any search for even the maid in another state.

She scrolled through the links Jason had

already viewed, relieved when pictures she found of herself reflected the distance she usually put between herself and the press. She rushed through the basics about Barrington's past, including pictures of him with his oldest and dearest friends from Harvard.

Bet he wouldn't set them up for murder.

Finally she got to the original murder accusations against Barrington. Before fleeing, she'd written them off as the paparazzi-generated, press nonsense her family had been subjected to all her life. She had never read what she assumed were all lies since it had never occurred to her that anyone had actually died. Panic had then forced her to flee without thinking things through. While fleeing, she hadn't had either the time or the opportunity to research anything.

Wait a minute. Those names…

She scrolled back up.

The list of victims included some of Barrington's oldest and dearest friends.

How could she have failed to pick up on at least that much before? Did she really have Asperger's syndrome after all? Or was it her aversion to anyone still breathing and therefore capable of her parents' shrillness and arguing?

When Barrington met his friends at the

polo club, he would insist that Veronica dress to the nines so he could show off his beautiful trophy wife, from such a fine old family. She'd manage a smile, never commit any of his friends' names to memory, and wander off to the club's deserted second floor. Ignoring whatever tendrils of conversation wafted up the broad staircase, she'd commune with faded pictures of past polo heroes in a warren of wainscoted halls. Those were the names Veronica remembered, those men in sepia tones with their hair parted down the middle, all safely dead.

But she also remembered how convinced she was that Barrington adored his Harvard friends. He always had his arms around them.

She had been scrolling without realizing it. Backing up, she read: "It is now believed that Veronica Hamilton's reason for arranging what was initially thought to be an accidental explosion aboard the yacht was to further her husband's business interests by effectively eliminating in a single stroke the entire board that would have opposed the merger of..."

She hadn't been aware of any of the particulars that followed since she'd never paid any attention to Barrington's business dealings. And it was only now that she read of Barrington's sorrow over the deaths of his friends, apparently expressed for the sake of the media.

The Barrington she'd left had only confirmed, with his indifference, her conviction that the servants' chatter about the murders was just nonsense out of the tabloids. Only interested in the past, she not only shunned the tabloids but any other source of news.

All these years she'd shared a bed, never with any great enthusiasm, she had to admit, with a man who would murder his oldest friends for a business merger?

And he'd known them for a lot longer than he'd known Veronica.

Cold terror crept over her. Tears threatened.

She looked up to see Jason looking at her steadily. As she watched, his pencil froze. The bottle of whiskey in his other hand, that he was about to put to his lips again, was returned to the table beside him instead. Idly, in the midst of everything else she had on her mind, she wondered why.

"What's wrong?" Jason asked.

She hadn't said a word. How could he tell? "Nothing."

He frowned. That she could see, but she hadn't frowned, so why had he? Then he stood and went into what she assumed was a kitchen since she soon heard a blender. He returned with a glass of something she tried to wave off, but he insisted she take it.

Jason swept an arm skyward. "The First Great Medicine Man of My People, from the time when the earth and the sky were as one, handed this recipe down through a thousand generations. However, some say he didn't include the Gatorade, the cheap whiskey, the Muscle Tech casein and whey formula, or the dash of Kool-Aid."

"*She* didn't include the Gatorade…" The same strength Veronica'd achieved when she saluted Toto The Cockroach bloomed again.

"A lowly squaw? Fine. The First Great Medicine *Person*. Now drink it. It'll either make you stronger or put you out of your misery."

Veronica forced some down. "The latter."

Jason folded his arms across his chest and tried to sound stern. "Drink it anyway."

It had one hell of a kick. How easy to slip away from every care, running down the hallways of Jason's drink.

She barely remembered to click out of those two purpled links and clear her browser history before putting aside the laptop and getting to her feet. The trailer was small, and there were no oil paintings of her ancestors or sepia-toned polo heroes, but there was Jason's art.

She found a hushed reverence in the Asian antiquities he'd used to construct the Kansas prairie and pointed to an ancient temple's exquisite spire. "What's this?"

"Indic-inspired example of what must be 11th-century vaulting technique since it survived Burma's 1975 earthquake."

"Wow!" Veronica was impressed and fascinated but beginning to wonder if she could stand straight. She looked up and imagined she could actually see something in another person's eyes. Jason's eyes were dancing.

"No more impressive," he said, "than your immediate knowledge of the Investment Company Act of 1940."

She laughed. "I almost choked to death at birth, born as I was with both a silver spoon and an annual report in my mouth. I was never interested in any of it but grew up knowing the bread and butter of the family business." Drunk! What had she just said? She may as well have clicked into 40 links about Barrington and mentioned that her real name was Veronica Hamilton while she was at it!

Jason wrapped a gentle arm around her. "You don't have to be alone with…whatever's troubling you."

Veronica yanked herself away so violently that she knocked his picture of the prairie off the wall. She wasn't sure why. Because she'd never trusted anyone, especially with her life? Or because Jason's gesture had so perfectly mimicked Barrington when he wrapped his arms around those he later killed.

This time she couldn't read what was in Jason's eyes as she escaped through his front door. "Sorry, but…it just occurred to me I really should go. Thanks for the use of the laptop."

She did hear what she took to be a rather lame attempt at humor before he shut the door behind her: "Tonto no touch white woman."

But back out in the dust of the street, with Eddie and his sidekick staring at her, all Veronica could think about was where she could possibly go, where she could possibly hide, to escape Barrington.

Betty Ann knew damn well there was only one person in the whole, great-big world she could trust, and she was—right now—lying on top of the jello-like mountain of flab that was his naked body.

As usual, Nesbitt was snoring.

"Nes, wake up! You always go to sleep after we do it!"

This caught Nesbitt mid-snore. His struggle to both wake up and finish the snore rocked Betty Ann's teeny trailer even more than their previous activities. Her boobs and his belly, still lubricated with sweat, slipped back and forth across each other with his efforts. It was like big Teutonic Plattes—or whatever them things underground were called—building up to one hell of an earthquake.

Finally little Betty Ann slipped off onto the floor. "Nes!"

"What is it, Lamb Chop?"

"We gotta talk."

"Talk? Oh. That."

"You know what I was telling you about the daughter who's onto me?"

"The daughter of the JFK assassin?"

"Well I'm smart enough to have figured out that she's not the real threat; it's the son-in-law, her husband."

"Threat? To you?"

"Big threat, Nes."

"There aren't any threats to you, Lamb Chop, not even little ones. At least not any that will live long." Nesbitt was fully awake now, every pound of him rippling behind his words.

Betty Ann licked some of the sweat off his thick neck, sexy and slow, then started licking her way down lower. In his case, there was a lot of territory to cover before they finally got down to business again. In the meantime Betty Ann was thinking: The assassin's daughter didn't know about Nesbitt. No one in Horwedel knew about Nesbitt because he didn't live there. He lived in Grundel, the closest town with a hotel he could work in. And he always hid his car and walked through the corn to the back of her trailer.

She'd seen him in a real-live professional wrestling match once. He was like one of those Japs. She couldn't remember the name. Subaru or something. Or was that that silly little car of his he could hardly fit into? Anyway, no one in or out of Horwedel could even touch her Nes from Grundel.

Betty Ann had a secret weapon. A big, bad, really dangerous secret weapon.

Jason stood alone amidst the endless emptiness of the prairie. But, though there were no other people with him, he knew the prairie was with him.

The wind caressed his face and ruffled his hair before moving off to blow the tall grasses up and down, a roiling, infinite ocean of green.

Something was tickling him. He looked down to see an officious-looking beetle crawling over his bare foot. It lingered with a leg arched in the air, swinging it this way and that as it worried over where to step next. Apparently it found the distances between Jason's toes annoying.

The sun soothed his bare back as he leaned over to yank up some arrowleaf balsam roots. He wiped them against his cut-off jeans and popped them into his mouth, savoring the strong hint of pine. The earth was warm and firm beneath his feet.

A lone meadowlark, breast as yellow as the corn would soon be, made an impossible landing in the tops of the tall grasses nearby. Jason knew its song as well as he knew the sound of his own voice: three phrases in a half-tone-downward progression that sounded as if the meadowlark was asserting, "It's me. It's me. It's me."

"Hacho," he greeted the bird softly.

Jason watched him pluck at a feather before taking off into the sparkling sunlight to soar back and forth above the thermals. How could any creature beneath this cosmic vault fail to grasp the infinity of time and space? He could even smell it in the vibrant air.

When he was little, white schoolteachers told him his people were from the North and had only been in Kansas for hundreds of years. Probably to justify their displacing them and worse. But his people were still alive then, to tell him they had wintered in this place of wind for a whole lot longer than that. Not only did "palefaces speak with forked tongue," but they didn't understand nomadic life.

"Hacho," he greeted the bird again, who landed even closer.

This time the meadowlark turned its head to look at him. Then it sang its announcement again, "It's me. It's me. It's me."

Jason answered softly, singing the next two notes in the downward half-tone progression, "And me."

When he was little, his people made up half the population of Horwedel, a town so isolated that its belief systems dated back decades, if not centuries. The father of Eddie, his tormentor, had considered Jason's mother fair game. There had been bad trouble after his uncle was beaten to death for stopping Eddie's father from raping Jason's mother.

By the time he was ten there was only his mother, his father, and his ancient Tali—his wizened grandmother who, in happier days, chased him with her feather duster to tickle his face. After his parents were gone, his Tali made him swear that he would do, or not do, whatever he had to in order to survive. And that he would never leave the land that, if it was anyone's, was theirs.

Now he was the last.

The beetle finally fell off the end of his big toe, somersaulting onto its back.

Jason had been a fool to think there could be any people in his life. He had been a fool to feel so sorry for a "paleface." He had disrespected his Tali's memory by sharing his sarcasm about the stereotypes attributed to his people with her. Because this "paleface" believed them.

He squatted to help the beetle right itself.

Then he regained his own feet in more ways than one. He smirked dismissively at the town behind him. He told himself it had only been because her tits were better than either Miss 300's or Betty Ann's. Then he looked back out across the endless emptiness of the prairie and let the wind wipe him clean.

Jason stood alone.

Veronica overheard Miss 300 telling her hubby that Jason hadn't shown up for work. Concerned for him, and oddly disappointed for herself, she had to force herself to pay attention to her call.

"Hello, my name is Vera Charbonneau, and I'm calling on a recorded line. May I speak to...to..." The interface between the automatic dialer and the computer system, both housed in the boss' office, was off again. The call had come through before her computer screen refreshed so she didn't have any account information. *Ah, finally. Corporate account.* "...to whomever is authorized to vote the shares for Winfield Savings & Loan?"

It sounded like it was going to take a while for the receptionist to figure out whether it would be the CFO, or the President, or perhaps the janitor. Veronica had time to think her situation over yet again.

She had to accept that there probably wasn't anywhere she could go where someone wouldn't eventually guess the truth. After a fitful night's sleep she had decided to stay in Horwedel, a teeny town with a job she could hold with a phony name. Fleeing would only confirm suspicions in Horwedel and expose her to more people's scrutiny elsewhere. Plus she didn't have enough money to run far.

Her parents, who probably wouldn't have helped her anyway, were dead. Of the legions of people she knew, mostly through Barrington, there wasn't one she could call a friend. What else could she do?

She was terrified, but Miss 300 had talked as if she wouldn't turn her in. Jason? He obviously made it his business to know a lot more about different times and places than anyone else in Horwedel. Drunk, she'd freaked, terrified of him at the time. In the clear light of a new day she might be deluding herself, but she couldn't even be sure he'd ID'd her.

"Ms. Charbonneau, are you still there? I'm still trying to get someone in Finance to confirm who's authorized to vote your proxy."

Back on hold, Veronica was surprised to realize how much she missed Jason's voice beside her, the one voice in that call center she didn't try to block out. She looked over at his desk, at leisure to examine the drawings he surrounded himself with since he wasn't there. Kansas. All Kansas. But no rusty metal siding. No weed-and-garbage-choked back yards decorated with old refrigerators. No trailers, not even his own. No people. She could relate to that.

It was all open prairie, as wide and vast as the open sea. As limitless as the night sky. Yet the drawings glittered with sunlight, despite the call center's dark interior.

Drawings of the tall grasses stood in rows, their folded bottoms taped to Jason's desk. When the call center's oscillating fan blew these drawings up and down, waves moved across a sea of grass.

For a moment Veronica thought she'd seen into the depths of Jason's eyes. Now she was sure she could see the intensity in each of his pencil strokes and feel how deeply he loved the prairie.

Despite all, she smiled broadly, and wondered if there were other drawings she couldn't see because he'd displayed them on the flimsy partition between their desks. Still on hold she found her headset had just enough slack to allow her to peek around the corner and froze.

There was one picture there that wasn't of Kansas. It was of her face. It was drawn so well that, despite her wig and make-up, any fool who'd seen even a distant shot of her in the media could have ID'd her.

"Ms. Charbonneau, it looks like I won't be able to get anyone to vote our shares with you over the phone today. Can I take your number and have someone call you back tomorrow?"

In a daze, Veronica gave out the number. Was there no safety? Was there no hope? Was there no escaping the detached and oblivious fool she'd been all her life? Then it hit her, out of left field. The answer that had eluded her like a mirage on her way from the gas station to Margret's trailer. And wiggled free of her grasp that night in the corn. Why did Barrington tip her off? Because nothing would better prove her guilt than if she tried, but of course failed, to hide.

Vaguely she heard Jason's friend, the wino, yelling at the boss to fix the computers. He was struggling with slow screens for his magazine sales too. Then Veronica heard the click as her call with the receptionist disconnected. This was immediately followed by the buzz in her ear announcing the next call, not surprising since Jason wasn't there to share the proxy calls. Nerves shot, she panicked, leaping into her script before the person who picked up even said hello, even though her screen hadn't refreshed.

"Hello, my name is Vera Charbonneau and I'm calling on a recorded line. May I speak to…to…" Screen still hadn't refreshed. She skipped ahead. "Recently you were mailed proxy material including a proxy card or voting instruction form to cast your vote at the upcoming meeting of shareholders to be held on—"

"*Veronica?!?!?*"

Finally her screen refreshed. She probably wouldn't have recognized the name alone but combined with the sound of his voice, she knew. It was a friend of Barrington's.

Her stomach turned; her mind screamed. It struck her that this guy wouldn't have been alive to ID her if he'd been a member of some board capable of curtailing Barrington's business dealings.

Hanging up on him wasn't enough. Veronica pulled the phone jack out of the wall.

Whatever that did to the control screens in his office, the boss reacted immediately. "Miss Share Beano," he sang out formally. The call center's incorrect spelling of her phony last name, combined with incorrect pronunciation, destroyed any beauty in the name Charbonneau. "What did you do now?" He ended with his usual speaking voice, what she imagined a sewer rat might sound like if screaming through a dreadfully tinny amplification system: "Crush your phone with one of them tits?"

"I'm…sick," she called out lamely. "I'm sorry. I'll have to leave for the day."

But as she bolted for the door, teeny Betty Ann suddenly hung up on the caller she was describing anal sex to, sprang out of her chair, and blocked Veronica's way out.

"You gonna tell us what that call was about…'Vera'?"

Why was she asking? Why was she shaking? Fear for "Vera"? Fury at "Vera"?

Veronica had been rich and beautiful. If she couldn't figure out what other people were feeling, it had been their problem, not hers. Investing in her wardrobe had always trumped worrying about even serious cognitive deficiencies.

But Betty Ann's emphasis on her phony name wasn't lost on her. Now Veronica's inability to read Betty Ann's eyes could cost her her life.

Oddly, it was Miss 300, the one she thought she had to fear, who brushed teeny Betty Ann aside and pulled her toward the door. "Come on, honey. I'll help you." Then she whispered loudly enough for everyone to hear, "You and I are in the same boat, you know. I told you we gotta stick together."

Once outside Veronica spotted Jason heading toward work at last. But he wasn't looking their way as he gazed sideways toward the prairie.

Miss 300 pulled her around the side of the call center and gave her hand a squeeze. "Listen, honey. I wish I could take you back to my place and fix you some ribs that'd fix you right up, but my hubby…" Miss 300 dropped Veronica's hand to tug at her own sleeve, trying to conceal a bruise. "Not only do both our hubbies cheat but mine…" She trailed off.

Same boat? Hubbies cheat? Miss 300 had said she knew who Veronica was, but was it possible that she didn't know about the murders? Veronica was lost. Except that this woman was yet another who knew who she was, and Veronica didn't know what to make of her. A hysterical sob escaped her.

Miss 300 wrapped a beefy arm around her. "There, there."

Again remembering how Barrington wrapped his arms around the people he later killed, she tried to jerk away.

Miss 300 held on tight. "I know it's hard."

Veronica stared blindly into Miss 300's eyes. How could she tell? How the fuck could she tell what this woman's intentions were? After all, she hadn't gotten it at all with Barrington. She struggled to free herself from Miss 300's huge arm again, in vain. Then, suddenly, she stopped fighting.

When she was very little, she had two nannies. Both said the same things, knowing the necessary script for their top-of-the-line jobs. But one was flighty and passive-aggressive; the other was genuinely kind and rock-steady. Veronica might not have been able to see the difference in their eyes, but she could feel it when they put their arms around her. Dared she rely on what she was feeling now? Miss 300's arm around her felt like the good nanny.

Then she felt Miss 300 shudder. "If I don't get back into the call center to answer the reception desk phones the boss, even though he's my hubby, will… Well, never mind. And don't you mind that small-fry Betty Ann. You just go on home and eat plenty and you'll be just fine."

Betty Ann was so damned scared. Dumb doctors said she didn't have to be, that she was just "paranormal," or whatever that dumb word was that meant scared when she didn't have to be. But she was smart enough to know they only said that because they were out to get her.

Damn Miss 300 for nosing into Betty Ann's business. Good thing Miss 300 didn't know her Nes from Grundel, or she'd probably tell him what Betty Ann did with her husband.

Betty Ann couldn't wait to talk to her Nes just as soon as she got out of work. It was all she could do to stop herself from running right over to interrupt him at work at the Grundel Hotel, right then and there. After all, he was the only one who knew what was really going on with the JFK assassination cover-up.

Damn that "Vera."

Dumb-injun Jason finally showed up for work. He took one of his dumb pictures down, real gentle like, and looked at it for a spell, like his friend, that dumb wino pushing magazines, might look at an empty bottle. Then he threw it in the trash, which was where all his dumb pictures belonged. What he didn't do, which he always did, was take out his flask.

Miss 300 answered a reception-desk call. Betty Ann was smart enough to leave her client breathing heavily while she eavesdropped.

"You're calling about one of our employees from…what 'regulatory agency'?" Miss 300 asked.

The boss was on her like fly paper, leaning over to hit Miss 300's mute button before hissing, "Whatever the fuck 'regulatory agency' they're from you better cooperate fully or your next bruises will be in places where all that flab can't protect you!" Then he un-muted.

"Certainly, sir," Miss 300 said into the phone. "The Horwedel Call Center always complies fully with all rules and regulations…"

The boss rolled his eyes heavenward,

raking his thick fingers through his greasy hair.

"…and all our paperwork is always in order." Miss 300 was looking at the boss for approval.

The wino was laughing so hard Betty Ann couldn't hear herself think.

"Sorry, sir. A little noisy here. I didn't get either the last name or the first name."

The boss gave the wino the evil eye and hit mute again to screech at his wife, "Rat them out. Sell them down the fucking river. You go soft on me, and you'll be missing an eye." He passed the lit end of his cigarette in front of Miss 300's face. "And repeat whatever they say so I can hear it." He unmuted.

"You say a person like myself could never understand such a name, so you're going to start by spelling the last name for me?" Suddenly there was an unmistakable look of complete, giddy relief on Miss 300's face as she repeated, "That's C-H-A-R-B-O-N-N-E-A-U?"

The cigarette was forgotten as both the boss and Miss 300 flipped their palms up and shrugged their shoulders. The boss wiped the sweat from his brow. Only that dumb injun still looked worried, very worried.

"Honestly, sir," Miss 300 continued in a completely convincing voice, "we've never even heard of anyone with a name like that."

The injun crossed his fingers for some dumb reason.

"You're welcome," Miss 300 said. "Sorry I couldn't help you. Goodbye."

Finally the injun relaxed too.

Miss 300 hung up the phone with a smile.

The boss actually smiled and patted Miss 300's shoulder. "And I thought Vera had a stupid last name. How would you pronounce this even stupider one, Char-bone-a-you?"

The injun was so dumb that he laughed at what Betty Ann thought was a pretty good shot at pronouncing the name the caller spelled for them. Then he went all serious and started carefully ripping something up in the trash, probably one of his dumb drawings. And people thought *she* was nuts?

Since that "regular" agency, or whatever it was called, hadn't been calling about anyone they knew, Betty Ann wasn't feeling quite as worked up any more. Still, as soon as she got out of work she was going to call her Nes in Grundel.

Veronica tried covering her ears to think, but she could still hear Margret's TV. The U.S. Department of Something or Other was again assuring the population that the rapidly enlarging "fourth star" in Orion's belt was nothing but light reflecting off a newly visible gas explosion in the Orion Nebula. Nothing to worry about since what they were seeing had happened a long, long time ago and was very far away. An elderly-sounding evangelical preacher in Mississippi was saying that was nothing but the old "weather balloon" cover up from the 1950s. With a particularly shrill voice, the preacher went on to say it was really the wrath of God coming straight at Earth because of interracial marriage. An esteemed colleague respectfully disagreed, certain it was the work of Mexican transsexuals.

To round out the presentation the network's aw-shucks human interest story featured testimonials by a bunch of first graders from an obscure town in Idaho. It was meant to be very cute since they were clearly the only people on the planet who were totally convinced it was an alien spacecraft.

Nothing about Barrington. No, wait…

Barrington had actually agreed to an interview? She heard his withering responses to some idiot's attempts to get him to answer irrelevant, gossip-mongering questions. But when the interviewer got to Veronica's whereabouts, she was astounded to hear Barrington open up, going on at length about how he was now completely convinced that she'd boarded that Paris flight after all. He then went on and on about how he'd told the police that any further search for her in this country was utterly useless.

Barrington clammed up again when the interviewer asked how Veronica could have entered France without a passport. "Mr. Hamilton, you said you personally found Mrs. Hamilton's passport and her purse left at JFK. All the other passengers on that flight, and their passports, have been accounted for."

Finally, apparently cornered, Barrington started in about phony passports and a report only he'd been privy to about rampant errors in French entry records. He then said he'd been "mistaken" about finding her passport anyway, and quickly changed the subject.

Veronica's heart skipped a beat. She knew she'd left her passport clearly visible at JFK. Was he protecting her? She started to cry, out of a heady combination of joy and relief. But something toyed with the back of her mind…

His voice. It sounded just like when he told her she should try and find her own personal legal counsel. Like a blind person with heightened hearing, a heightened sensitivity to the nuances in a human voice came screaming out of her subconscious.

His friend must have told him where she was. Knowing that, he no longer wanted the authorities to find her first. Whatever his reasons were, he wasn't trying to protect her.

She may never have understood other people or paid them much attention, but she now knew enough about Barrington to justify the sinking feeling that turned into wrenching nausea. Although it wasn't cold, she couldn't stop shivering, even when she held her knees tightly against her chest. The reason she couldn't think wasn't Margret's TV. The reason she couldn't think was because there was no longer anything to think about.

Barrington? With all his ruthlessness and all the resources at his disposal? What could she do to save herself? Hitchhike till his legions of unscrupulous underlings paid off enough people to find someone who could rat her out? Run as far as she could across the prairie till bloodhounds tracked her down?

All she ever wanted was to witness beauty. Like the night sky in Kansas. Now the most she could hope for was a life in prison. Maybe just one, amidst all the people she'd snubbed and ignored and never understood, would occasionally mail her a postcard of something beautiful.

Like a cold, wet dog seeking the warmth of a fire, she unzipped her suitcase, and savored the last of the luxuries she'd allowed herself to pack:

The first was a beautiful silk scarf, exquisitely embroidered with teeny Asian temples. With its pale, pearly background Veronica had never once dared to wear it, lest she mar its perfection with even a speck of dirt.

The second was the most beautiful book she'd ever read. *À la recherche du temps perdu.* Marcel Proust. In the original French. *Du côté de chez Swann.* She knew the exact page she wanted: "A young woman whose pensive face and elegant veils did not suggest a local origin…drawing from her resigned hands long and uselessly elegant gloves."

"Shishum?"

"Yes, His*tus?*"

He was gratified to have his out-of-style preference for the masculine ending of his name honored, even if she had included a note of sarcasm. *It* had included a note of sarcasm, if he was going to honor Shisha-now-Shishum's preference for the neuter. "Third planet out from the star isn't much bigger than our ship," he sent first, gearing up for his punchline, but *it* interrupted.

"Us," it sent.

"As in we're now the ship? Yes, not much bigger than us," he corrected. "But it's liquid H_2O!"

"Not possible," it sent back. "Apparently we're still not close enough for the joke that is our only remaining chemical analysis program. Begging your pardon, since you are now our only remaining chemical analysis program."

"Ironic for the First in Command," Histus sent back, "but at least you, the Second in Command, are the much-farther-reaching communications program."

"Those few of us who survived by uploading ourselves had no time to choose what part of the ship we became."

"True," he sent, reflecting that no good came from its dwelling on the slaughter of every last one of their kind, even their own bodies, over and over again.

"So," it sent, "we must accept that what we became didn't reflect our hierarchy, like accepting we no longer have the bodies that justify our thinking of ourselves as either one sex or the other?"

Ouch. Shisha…no, Shish*um*…could get on his nerves, but he was going to ignore that. "Back to the third. Why 'not possible' that it's liquid H_2O?"

"I've been studying their transmissions," Shishum sent. "It isn't any kind of gas or liquid—not to mention lethal H_2O that would—think about it—tend to preclude there being anything alive to send transmissions. Remarkably, it's solid! Its pathetically few life forms have had to evolve appendages they use to drag themselves across the surface. They live their whole lives flattened against the surface by gravity, completely unable to move down into the planet itself."

"Hard to believe," he sent back. "Still, I concede I'm at the very edge of my range so I'll check again. But if I'm right and Translate misinterpreted their transmissions—I mean, who ever heard of a rock supporting life, and Translate's inaccuracies are legendary—this raises a legal question. Have they received 'Eclipse Beats'?"

"Not yet, not with their primitive methods of communication, but soon," it sent.

Primitive indeed. Teeny lifeforms snapped like magnets onto a teeny rock planet? What could they be made of to withstand such a fate? Were they solid too? Absurd. Shame none of his kind had uploaded into Translate. The planet probably was liquid H_2O, though Histus couldn't imagine a lifeform that could survive that either.

"How long are we legally obligated to give them to figure out it's a song before we can write them off as 'sub' and mine their H_2O?"

"Depends on their communication capacities," Shishum sent.

"Research it all. If we're going to fuel our ship by wiping out a planet supposedly transmitting, we've got to be able to document their stupidity in failing to identify our hail as a song before we kill them all."

Betty Ann could hear the boss arguing about how long it took the computer screens to refresh for outgoing calls with that damned wino peddling magazine subscriptions. The wino was saying it was because that moonlighting SETI guy made them wireless with technology designed to reach the stars, not the next state. Betty Ann was smart enough to know they had to be wireless to get the only kind of business they could get: spillover that got farmed out to them illegally from "real" call centers.

The boss kept yelling about how the fancy hardware the SETI guy had sold them, pirated from NASA, should be able to handle anything. Finally the wino said something that pissed him off so bad that the boss stormed out of the call center.

Betty Ann didn't care since she was on incoming. What the hell would she do with client names? Find their wives and rat them out? But she was also smart enough to know they were totally missing the point about the dangers of using shit that was supposed to pick stuff up from outer space. On the other hand, she hadn't heard *him* between calls lately. Maybe, at least for now, extraterrorists were one less thing she had to worry about.

Which brought her back to the JFK assassin. Thankfully her current client thought her whimper of fear was her getting turned on by his grunting.

Did the daughter know that when her father was a kid he'd killed JFK, or did she just think that letter Betty Ann sent her father was crazy? Would she get enough advance notice to be able to tell Nes so he could protect her from the real threat, the daughter's killer husband? Betty Ann was smart enough to know the husband knew what his wife's father had done, and liked it.

"Lamb Chop!"

Lamb Chop? Her client didn't sound like Nes, but calling her Lamb Chop was enough to get Betty Ann thinking about her Nes in other ways. Sometimes Grundel was too damn far away.

Even with her client whooping as he got his rocks off like a laughing henna, one of those funny-looking African dogs, Betty Ann could hear a ruckus out on the street. Sounded like Eddie and Ike, them no-goods that didn't have to work and had nuthin' better to do than hang out on the street and pick on the injun. Dumb injun didn't know he was all growed up and could take them scrawny old buzzards easy. But the injun was inside the call center…

Eddie was screaming something about a car just as Betty Ann heard it pulling up.

The door to the call center all but busted open.

Miss 300 looked up. "Well la de da."

The man standing in the doorway was dressed in—what were them things?—pinned stripes, like British royalty. Betty Ann thought maybe she'd seen that face somewhere. Maybe he was the king of fucking London but no one in Horwedel, except that blind old bat Margret, watched the news. And maybe he wasn't, because that was the most god-awful, beat-up old pinky ring Betty Ann had ever seen.

She watched the way the man stared through Miss 300, his cold blue eyes as calm and quiet as a loaded gun. She just knew this was the kind who would walk over dead bodies to get what he wanted.

Betty Ann was smart enough to know those were a killer's eyes.

Her headset buzzed in her ear, announcing her next client. She didn't even check to be sure the boss was still gone before hanging up. Real quiet-like, she took her headset off. All she wanted was to run to her Nes in Grundel, but that murderer was blocking the door. So Betty Ann started backing slowly away from the door, deeper into the call center. Even the injun, watching the killer like a hawk as she passed his cubicle, looked murderous.

The killer jarred the floor with the sharp, jerky steps he took to get to Miss 300. Betty Ann could feel them through her own feet and lower legs. They felt like blows to the gut.

"Do you have an employee named Vera Charbonneau?"

"Share Beano?" Miss 300 answered, suddenly wide-eyed.

"Close enough."

Miss 300 bit her lip and darted a look toward the boss' office. Miss 300 looked scared, real scared. She kept darting looks from the boss' office to a pack of cigarettes her hubby must have left on her reception desk. Betty Ann remembered seeing cigarette burns on Miss 300 when she scratched up under her blouse once and thought no one was looking.

But then Miss 300 gave "Vera's" desk a soft, sad look and stiffened her jaw. Still it took a while for her to get the word out: "No."

"You don't mind if I look around?"

Miss 300 looked worried sick. Betty Ann could smell her gas problem going crazy, even from as far away as Betty Ann was.

The killer held a white handkerchief to his nose but leaned in close to Miss 300. "Does the name Barrington Hamilton mean anything to you?"

Miss 300 was quick about saying "no" this time.

"I thought not," said the killer. Then he did something that made Betty Ann shiver. He smiled. And put a hand on Miss 300's shoulder. He even pocketed the handkerchief. "You know that nasty regulatory agency that called yesterday looking for…Vera?"

Miss 300 looked confused.

The killer, watching her like a hawk, narrowed his eyes. "Vera C-H-A-R-B-O-N-N-E-A-U?"

Miss 300's eyes snapped really wide.

"I'm just trying to help her by finding her before they do. I'm her husband."

Miss 300 looked like she didn't believe him.

Betty Ann couldn't help screaming out loud.

The injun gave her a real nasty look and put his finger to his lips.

"Vera's" husband nailed her with his eyes, freezing her blood, then looked back at Miss 300. "I can understand your wanting to protect…Vera…from the authorities that are after her. She's a sweet girl. But I'm one of the good guys."

It was all Betty Ann could do to stop herself from whimpering out loud. "Vera's" husband! So this was the one she really had to fear, the one who knew his wife's father killed JFK. The same one who killed Betty Ann's parents, though she hadn't even told Nes how this killer had arranged that traffic accident when Betty Ann drove a car for the last time before the state took her license away. If only she could get past the killer to that door, she'd run all the way to Grundel. In Grundel her Nes would know what to do to make sure this killer could never again be a threat to anyone.

Betty Ann backed up until she hit the wall and then did all she could to press herself into it. Without taking her eyes off the killer, she ran her hands up and down the back wall's cinderblocks, feeling for something— anything—to protect herself. She knocked over a pail, and set something to rolling across the floor in front of her. When she darted a look, she saw that it was only paper towels.

She could see Miss 300 was shaking with fear, though Betty Ann knew Miss 300 didn't know who this murderer was. She was afraid of what her hubby would do to her later.

But Miss 300 still got out, "I'm sorry, mister, I'd like to help you. But I don't know anyone named Vera C-H-A-R whatever the rest of that was."

Betty Ann was gasping for air and starting to feel dizzy, and her hands were jerking about—real spastic like—on the wall behind her. Then she felt something hard and real heavy. She took a quick look. Tool of some kind. Pipe wrench? Maybe too heavy for anyone her size to even pick up.

She was also smart enough to know the murderer husband was just testing Miss 300. He knew his wife "Vera," who Betty Ann had always been smart enough to know was the daughter of the JFK assassin, was there. But then the killer looked at Betty Ann again, and all she knew was that suddenly the pipe wrench was in her hands and her hands were behind her back.

The killer stomped towards her.

Betty Ann's fingers tightened around the wrench.

The killer checked all the cubicles.

That gave her the time she needed to think again. He already knew his wife worked at the call center, though she'd left for the day, lying about being sick. Why'd she leave and

not tell him? What was going on with that
phony regular agency, or whatever, that must
have been how…how what? Wait a minute.
It was all so confusing; it was making her head
hurt. That regular agency, that must have
been how he found his wife. Was she really
trying to escape her husband like the actress
Betty Ann had gotten Miss 300 to believe
"Vera" was? Something wasn't adding up, but
there was no time for it now. He definitely
knew where Betty Ann was, and he'd already
killed her parents because she had sent that
letter to his father-in-law, JFK's killer. So if
he knew where Betty Ann was, why was he
checking all the desks?

Suddenly the wino stood swaying in front
of her, drunker than she'd ever seen him. The
injun hadn't taken his flask back all day. The
wino started one of his long speeches but little
Betty Ann elbowed him aside with so much
scared, crazy force that he sprawled across the
floor.

The killer was getting closer, about to
walk past Jason's desk when he spotted all the
injun's dumb pictures and slowed. When he
got to the partition between the injun's desk
and "Vera's," he stopped. Once again the
killer sent a shudder up Betty Ann's spine by
smiling. "I say, that's fine work, old sport."

Without saying a word, Jason turned toward the killer with a look that sent another shiver up her spine.

But the killer had already moved on to his wife's desk. Frowning, he picked up that ratty postcard "Vera" was always looking at. He was about to flip it over when the door opened and a man in a servant's uniform scurried over to him with one of them big fancy phones. The killer dropped the postcard to take the phone and look at its screen.

The servant shifted from one foot to the other before speaking. "I did precisely as you requested, Mr. Hamilton, and booked you a room in the closest available hotel, which you can see on the map. But you couldn't possibly spend the night in...such a place."

The killer squinted at the phone and put his handkerchief to his nose again. "The town's named *Grundel?*"

"Yes, sir. Are you sure you want me to leave you alone in Grundel while I have the car seen to? Begging your pardon, sir, but that minor maintenance can wait and—"

"Do precisely as you're instructed. I'll get whatever I need out of the locals, trust me."

They made a beeline for the door, la-de-da "Mr. Hamilton" now so oblivious to his

surroundings that he knocked the two folding
chairs in reception over without noticing.
Betty Ann figured they would have walked
right over Miss 300 if she'd been in front of
the door.

When they were gone, Miss 300 devoured
half a bag of cheese doodles in a single gulp.
Then she fetched a fanzine from under her
table and flipped through a few pages of the
latest celebrity news till she found the page
she wanted. "That man didn't look anything
like her husband. You can't fool me. I know
everything."

Buzz. Heavy breathing. "Lamb Chop!"
Veronica hit mute and yelled in the boss'
direction, "I'm getting incoming 900 again!"

"What'd ya do this time, Share Beano, hit
the wrong desktop icon with one of them tits?
Transfer to Betty Ann."

"She just took a call."

"Miss 300?"

"She just got a call too." Veronica
paused, piecing things together although she
could only hear Miss 300's side of the
conversation. The police were looking for a

missing person. Veronica choked.

So, this was finally it. At least Barrington had changed his mind and was letting the police pick her up instead of coming after her himself. With luck, she wouldn't get the death penalty. But Miss 300's next words brought a giddy rush of temporary relief.

"It's about a man!" Veronica shouted toward the boss' office, "…who supposedly stopped here yesterday before spending the night in Grundel. He hasn't been seen since."

Why did Betty Ann jerk her skinny neck around to stare at her? But no point dwelling on that since she figured Betty Ann wouldn't give her the time of day, let alone an explanation.

Still talking to the police, Miss 300 turned to gaze at her too. Veronica tensed, since she wasn't able to figure out what the look in Miss 300's eyes meant either. Maybe her yells to the boss were too loud? Miss 300 started to shake but told the police she hadn't seen the man. From what Veronica could overhear, the police were confirming over and over again that Miss 300 had been in the call center all day and that she hadn't seen the man. Veronica figured the boss couldn't help the police either since she'd already overheard that he, like Veronica, had been out most of yesterday. She tried to yell at the boss more quietly, to avoid disturbing Miss 300. "It sounds like she'll be on the phone for a while."

"Oh for fuck's sake," barked the boss. "Transfer your incoming 900 call to me."

Soon the wino, closer to the boss' office, was rolling with laughter. All Veronica could hear was that the boss was talking in falsetto.

Not for the first time that morning, she felt Jason looking her way. But every time she turned to smile back at him she found he wasn't looking at her. Instead he was looking at the drawing on the partition between them that she now knew was of her, even if she couldn't see it.

Remembering those purpled links on Jason's laptop and the accuracy with which he'd drawn her, she figured Jason must have ID'd her. But, sadly, it no longer mattered if everyone in Horwedel ID'd her. She'd been spared for now; the police were only looking for some random missing person who'd passed through. But it was only a matter of time.

Her stomach turned. How sad that the best she could hope for was a prison sentence for Barrington's murders.

On autopilot she fielded a shareholder

call.

At least Jason hadn't turned her in. Would he remember her, keep her picture, when she was gone? She would remember him.

Lunch time. Veronica turned toward Jason. She wanted to offer him some of the better-than-usual meal she'd made while she was home from work the day before. Maybe she could ask him which direction she should walk in to get to the magnificent open prairie of his drawings, a world that did not include the likes of Barrington Hamilton. But he was already gone, exiting the call center with just a few long strides.

She felt a hefty arm enclose her. "Come on, honey," Miss 300 whispered in her ear. "I got lunch all fixed up nice." She nodded in the direction of Betty Ann, who slipped into the boss' office. "My hubby won't be wantin' none of it."

Who was Veronica to turn up her nose at free food? The lunch she'd brought could be saved for another day.

The dust swirled about their feet as they crossed some old railroad tracks behind the call center and she looked up to see a part of Horwedel she'd never seen before. Its two trailers were newer and bigger. She smiled vaguely to herself about having at least made it to the right side of the tracks.

Two men bolted out of the first trailer. She recognized them as Jason's tormentors, Eddie and the other one whose name she'd never heard, who were always out on the street. They looked old and frail, so she never understood why Jason tolerated it. The one whose name she didn't know, carrying a dog-eared girlie magazine as usual, whistled at her as usual.

Miss 300 led her to the second trailer. It was pink. "I have so much to show you," said Miss 300 happily, her flyaway hair fluttering about. She shooed Veronica into the trailer like a chicken into a coop.

A crocheted moose's head, encrusted with grease, hung over the stove. An eye that had started to unravel was half hanging out, suggesting the moose had died in a horrible accident.

Lime-green plastic doilies and bobble-headed Betty Boops were everywhere. But the focal point was what could only be described as a shrine to her marriage to the boss. Rows of almost identical pictures showed them on their wedding day, documenting every bite of cake.

"Isn't it beautiful?" Miss 300 asked.

Veronica stared at Miss 300's eyes, wishing she could determine if she was being sarcastic.

"Now don't be all silent, like I know you can be," Miss 300 went on, "especially when you've got things on your mind. You're at home in this here heaven; you can let it all hang out." As if to demonstrate she reached up to pop the moose's eye back in, exposing a tsunami of flab usually concealed by her top. It was cascading over the top of the maternity pants she wore, though Veronica was pretty sure she wasn't pregnant.

Lunch featured grease with a side of ribs, Twinkies, pink Snowballs, and multi-colored jello cubes Veronica suspected would glow in the dark. But it was a break from her usual white rice.

"Thank you," she managed, after choking down a single rib.

Miss 300 responded with a greasy hand on top of hers. "Honey, I'll always be your…guardian. I'll always take care of you. I told you we had to stick together."

Veronica couldn't imagine what commonality could have prompted this, and was afraid to draw attention to her own situation by asking, but she was grateful. Choking back her own agonies, she managed to smile at Miss 300 and put her other hand on top of Miss 300's.

Miss 300 continued. "There's something I have to tell you about yesterday. I tried to get out to walk to Margret's to tell you last night, but my hubby…"

Something so important that Miss 300 felt it couldn't wait till Veronica returned to work the next day? All acceptance of her fate gone, Veronica jolted back, clutching her own throat. She remembered stupidly talking before hearing the voice of Barrington's friend, instead of waiting for her computer screen to refresh. A pathetic little sound, something between a whimper and a scream, escaped her.

Miss 300 grabbed her hand again and gave it a squeeze. "Well… That phone call I got today… Maybe what happened yesterday don't matter no more. Maybe it's all been taken care of."

"What doesn't matter anymore?" Veronica asked, her voice cracking, tears threatening, and the hand Miss 300 held shaking. Where had her quiet resignation gone?

"There, there," Miss 300 crooned, patting her hand. "Nothing, it was just…a joke, honey, don't you worry now. How about another nice rack of ribs?"

"No…thanks." Veronica was still shaking. Eating even one rib had been a mistake; her stomach knotted tightly around it. She fought back a dry heave.

Miss 300 brushed some hair out of Veronica's face and straightened her collar before asking, "What did your mama use to give you for comfort?"

"Painfully shrill screaming." Veronica smirked, which made her feel better.

"They all do that."

Veronica surprised herself by blurting out, "Not like mine!"

"Aw, honey, I shouldn't be telling someone as fancy as you something like this…" Miss 300 trailed off, struggling to straighten her own hair. "But I can't stand for you to feel bad, so I will tell you if it makes you feel any better."

Why the hesitation? "Tell me what?"

"My mama used to get all liquored up. Then she'd beat me till she broke whatever part of me wasn't padded well enough yet to protect me. There, I can see it in your eyes. Your mama didn't do that, did she?"

"No," said Veronica, noting Miss 300's blush. "But my mother called me into the formal reception room on my seventh birthday and—"

"That was a bad thing?"

"Unless we had guests, the family never used the formal reception room except for bad things." Veronica closed her eyes, and the 19th-century words she'd been taught as a child spilled out. "It lent grandeur to formal announcements, typically of my parents' eternally imminent, but never actual, divorce."

Miss 300 sounded confused. "But this time it was for a fancy birthday party?"

Veronica kept her eyes shut. She could see that 19th-century room, beautiful only when empty, dead and devoid of shrillness. "No one celebrated my birthday. Mother called me in to lend grandeur to her announcing that I was to marry for money." She choked on the last word. "All I had known was the honor and romance of the 19th century. Mother informed me that the only reason she hadn't aborted me was because they needed a new infusion of wealth in the family—old money, nothing as gauche as new, of course. And that I was honor-bound to—"

"But my mama said marriage is the biggest compliment a girl can get!" Miss 300 squeezed her hand hard.

Veronica's eyes snapped open to an onslaught of pictures of the boss, leering at her behind Miss 300's pathetically bowed back. "Your mama was wrong!"

"What?"

"Your mama…along with my parents, everyone alive in the 19th century, and even myself…were all wrong! Those of use born in subsequent centuries erred in thinking we could still live in the 19th, in thinking that marriage was the ultimate—"

"My mama told me she'd be stuck with me for life cuz I was too damn ugly for any man to marry. Sure fooled her, didn't I?"

Veronica deflated, realizing she wasn't being understood and not even sure she understood herself. "Uh…well, yes, I suppose you did."

"But this all started with my asking what your mama gave you for comfort."

"Nothing."

"Well, then, we gotta start making up for lost time. When my mama was done beating me she'd always throw me a big bag of cheese doodles to cork up my fussin'. So I knew the minute I got that first handful in my mouth it was over, my mama was an angel, and I was safe." Miss 300 pushed a bowl of cheese doodles across the table toward Veronica. "Those of us with husbands like ours have got to be guardian angels for each other."

"Thanks." Veronica forced herself to eat a cheese doodle. Why the claim of commonality when their husbands couldn't differ more? Again she dared not ask but had to concede that, of the two of them, it may have been a close contest, but the one who had fared better in marriage was Miss 300.

Soon they traipsed back over the railroad tracks to work. Veronica peered into Miss 300's eyes, trying to force herself into being able to figure out what the meaning of their lunch together had been. When she finally gave up, she looked past Miss 300 to concentrate on something she could understand, the beauty of the sun sparkling in the fields beyond the town.

Back in the call center Jason hadn't returned yet, so she thought she'd steal another look at the drawing of her he'd been looking at all morning. But, again, she was surprised.

He must have replaced it the day before when she wasn't at work. There was no picture of Veronica anywhere. She had been replaced by a beautifully rendered picture of a bird with a yellow breast.

Shame burned her cheeks as she remembered how she'd been thinking about Jason that morning. What a vain, presumptuous fool. She understood other people so little.

She took her first call. Her screen refreshed immediately. It wasn't anyone Barrington knew. It wasn't an Incoming 900 call that should have gone to Betty Ann. As if all that wasn't impressive enough, it was a Tenants in Common registration, but both people were at home and agreed on how to vote.

All systems worked perfectly for another six calls, back-to-back since Jason hadn't returned to share Outgoing Proxy with her.

Veronica saw what she assumed was the explanation when a man wheeling a metal suitcase with a NASA logo exited the boss' office, followed by the boss carrying an old piece of equipment he dumped next to a garbage can. Veronica saw Miss 300 wink at her. Veronica saw the exquisite interplay of light and shadow in the gardens of Versailles when she went back to gazing fondly at her postcard from M. Charbonneau.

Veronica heard Jason returning to his seat. Veronica heard Betty Ann scream, "*He's* back, between the calls!" Veronica heard the shareholder she was speaking with disconnect their call, and was just thinking that there might now be some space between her calls with Jason present, when she suddenly saw and heard no more.

At first she thought she'd fainted. What else would explain an instant loss of every sense such that she didn't even know which direction was up? But the term "blackout" didn't apply because even seeing black implied seeing something. The closest she could come to describing what she saw was that she was looking through clear glass at an infinity of clear glass with nothing behind it. Terrified, she asked herself, *am I dead?* But she'd never believed in an afterlife, so the ability to ask the question put that fear to rest.

Buzz. Her computer screen indicated a corporate account. Everything was back to normal. She noticed Miss 300 was still looking at her. When the person on the phone put her on hold to get the person authorized to vote the shares, Veronica called out to Miss 300, "Did you see me do anything strange between my last call and this one?"

"No, you was just staring at your postcard like always."

The person on the phone came back to say that the person authorized to vote wasn't available, took a message, and ended the call.

Again, everything vanished. Veronica had never felt so completely, agonizingly, alone.

Not only was her whole world gone, but all the senses she used to perceive it were too. Then, ever so slowly, a new feeling crept over her: What if this wasn't a void? What if she was in the middle of another place that might be as crowded as the call center? But she didn't have a single sense that allowed her to perceive it.

Buzz. IRA registration through an investment advisor. The shareholder probably didn't even know which fund it was in. "Whatever you're selling," said a shrill woman's voice, "I'm not interested and I'm going to hang up on you now." Click.

An even eerier feeling crept over Veronica this time. What if she did have the senses with which to perceive this place but just…wasn't paying attention to them? She thought about blind people having acute hearing and tried to get as far away from the senses she was used to depending on as possible. But trying not to think of them just made her think of them more. And what kinds of things was she looking for instead? What other senses could possibly exist?

Buzz. Typical joint tenancy registration. Either person could vote for both. Veronica had reached the wife. While taking the vote she looked around. More or less normal.

Betty Ann was whimpering about an "extraterrorist," and even Miss 300 was trying to comfort her, it was true, but Betty Ann always thought someone or something was after her. Over her phone call all Veronica could hear from the wino was "this ship Earth, hurtling through a constant night" and something about "two ships passing," but he seemed agitated too. However she also noticed that the wino was a whole hell of a lot drunker than usual. It wasn't until she turned toward Jason that she saw something really out of the ordinary.

She could see a new drawing. It wasn't of the prairie, or a bird, or anything at all that she could recognize.

The wife's vote was finished. Click.

And there she was again, still thinking about Jason's drawing. Suddenly it was as if her eyes were adjusting to the dark, but it wasn't her eyes exactly. Was it her imagination, like seeing what she was thinking about superimposed on a dark room, or was she actually surrounded by what Jason had drawn?

At first she was startled and afraid, because all the circles she'd seen in Jason's drawing were right next to her, so much so that they almost seemed to be inside her. But then she realized there was nothing in the distance. No depth perception. Not even dimension. Some instinct told her she was looking at spheres, but they all appeared flat because there was no shadowing or shading. Every color was deep and pure, with no gradations. Finally she realized what was missing. She was neither "seeing" with, nor could she see, any form of light.

Buzz. Another corporate. Should she put this receptionist on hold and call out to the boss to stop the calls? No. What was she thinking? Anyone who balked at taking the next call or hung up on a call—even if the world was coming to an end—could be fired without mercy. With the possible exception of Betty Ann because she was putting out.

Besides, the glare of light in the call center was now agonizing, a million times worse than coming out of a dark room into the full light of day. And she was beginning to sense again, in that other place, that vast quiet of a night sky that she'd first sensed when she felt there was just a hint of something strange between the calls. She wanted to know what all those circles were. Veronica realized she hadn't said a word just as the receptionist said, "Well, I don't like the strong, silent type, but I do thank you for not breathing heavily."

Click.

Motion. Very slow but it was there. She hadn't picked it up before. But she was moving, and so were all the circles.

"They're sending. But their messages are blank. And their aim is off."

"What did they hit?" Histus sent back.

"One of our exterior sensors," Shishum answered.

"Blank? They said nothing?"

"Nothing."

"And they received 'Eclipse Beats'?"

"Finally."

"And the same place on the planet that received 'Eclipse Beats' sent back the blank messages?"

"Well…"

Histus waited, remembering with irritation the last time the former Shisha quite literally bumped into him when they both still had bodies. Hardly the Second in Command of his dreams.

"…that was hard to establish. What they sent didn't even come to us directly but ricocheted all over the place. Both off other locations in…or, in their case, on…the planet and off some of the junk they have orbiting it. I'm not even sure they meant to contact us at all."

"Shishum, we have to be clear on everything before we can legally destroy life on their planet. But your reference to 'on' the planet wasn't lost on me and I must first reconfirm its chemical composition."

"The blank messages are coming from just one location, not the location that finally received 'Eclipse Beats,' but very close."

"And you've documented all you can about their primitive communications system?" Histus sent.

"Yes."

"Then we should be set."

When the work day ended Veronica wanted to ask Jason about his new drawings, for now there were many. All included the circles she herself had at last "seen." But he had later added wispy, ephemeral-looking tendrils, which she had not seen, that connected the circles. Veronica, however, was stuck on a call with a long-winded shareholder, and Jason again disappeared too quickly. So instead she alone stepped gingerly into the daylight outside the call center.

The light that normally caused her no problem now ricocheted wildly off everything. She squinted till her eyes were almost shut, but it was of little help; she could hardly see. By the time she got to Margret's trailer a raging headache threatened to split her skull. When she got into her room she yanked the window curtain shut and curled up on her bed with all the covers wrapped tightly over her eyes.

Margret's TV was, as usual, blaring.

"And in continuing coverage of our top story, commentary is streaming in from all over the world in the wake of a Kansas SETI facility's announcement that after waiting in vain since the middle of the last century it has at last received a transmission that proves the existence of extraterrestrial intelligence."

In a heartbeat Veronica was out of her room and in the living room, seated next to Margret, who was muttering something about it being the end of the world.

An overly made-up news commentator who looked like a Ken doll was trying to look serious. "So, Candy, for those of us like myself who don't exactly keep up on this kind of thing, what does SETI stand for?"

"The Search for Extra Terrestrial Intelligence." Candy was clearly reading off a teleprompter. A Malibu Barbie if there ever was one, her make-up threatened to crack when she smiled to show off a row of glisteningly white, capped teeth.

Veronica turned to Margret. "What was the message? Did it include imagery? Something with circles?"

"No, nobody said nuthin' about no pictures. Jus' some kinda code scientists say it'll take years to figure out."

"This just in," announced the Ken doll. "SETI is no longer denying that the message came from the direction of the 'fourth star' in Orion's belt, though they still claim there's been an error in calculating the distance, which is now shown as much too close to us to come from another star system."

"And in other news," Candy continued, "Ditching the baby nurse, choosing a name, shopping for the nursery—inside Kate's final preparations. Our exclusive celebrity baby countdown next!"

Margret pushed past Veronica impatiently, mumbling about death and destruction on her way to the bathroom. Veronica saw the salmon light of sunset starting to streak the walls and left the trailer.

Outside the oncoming darkness was kinder to her eyes. She picked her way through the garbage, past the rusting refrigerator in Margret's yard, and out onto the open fields. She could see that the corn was getting bigger and, as the sun finally set, she could also see that this was true of the new star in Orion's belt.

What were those circles? Where had they come from? Veronica closed her eyes, trying to remember them as the post-sunset breeze bathed her face with the cool clarity of a splash of water. One huge circle. Few really little circles. Two much bigger circles. Two medium-sized circles.

Spheres, not circles. A solar system, but not just any solar system, *the* solar system, *her* solar system. Veronica's eyes snapped open, looking straight at Orion's "fourth star."

If Histus still had a body, he could at least have escaped Shishum by going to sleep. It was looking for something but, rather than waiting to send to Histus until it found whatever it was looking for, Shishum sent to

Histus first. Then it bored on endlessly, reporting all the things it wasn't looking for that it came across while searching.

"No, that's not it… Ah. Here. What it is is that I made a mistake."

"Were you thinking that you might, at some point, tell me what that mistake was?" Histus sent back, regretting his loss of temper as soon as he did so. Especially when Shishum didn't respond.

But, to his own surprise, he then sent even worse: "Shisha, your incompetence has flown to new depths. If you don't tell me immediately, I will be forced to appoint a new Second in Command."

"You remember when I told you I'd set you up with a direct communications link with the location where we sent 'Eclipse Beats'?"

Histus was remembering similar conversations with Shisha, going back to when they both had bodies, and such conversations did put him to sleep. To try to escape this sudden, dangerous rage of his he tried to concentrate on what it felt like to sleep now. He remembered his wing relaxing, then gently falling downward through shifting currents of gravity. He tried to feel the different caresses as each stratum of gasses tried to hold him, then softly released him.

"I made a mistake. I linked you to the location sending blank messages instead. It's close but—"

Histus interrupted. "Close? Do you think for one wing stroke that 'close' will save all that's left of our species? I'm 'close'—very, very close now—to being able to confirm that you weren't close at all when you came up with your silly idea about a rock planet supporting life. But I won't send to you until I'm sure, not close."

Shishum sent no more.

In between calls Veronica struggled to see if she could detect the moon orbiting the Earth. *Any moment the police or Barrington could show up, and I will never behold this wonder again.* But just when she thought she'd spotted the moon, she found herself back in Horwedel. No click. No call.

Looking around, Veronica saw no one was on a call. And no one—recent experiences giving actual validity to this particular expression—was off in outer space, either. Miss 300 was at Betty Ann's desk.

The boss came out of his office. "Yes, geniuses, I did something I never, ever do. I turned the calls off. And yes, Betty Ann is taking a 'mental health day.' But that's where this fucking shit stops. You geniuses may not know this but personally I don't care what you do in between calls. Eat all Miss 300's junk food. Eat each other. Sleep with your eyes wide open like you've been doing lately. As long as that buzz wakes you up when you get a call I don't care. But the next person who wastes my time telling me they *think* they've got something wrong with them medically, or that we're in contact with extraterrestrials, will walk out of my office *knowing* they've got something wrong with them medically." He started back to his office, but an independent phone rang at the empty reception desk. After checking the caller ID he answered with saccharin sweetness, "Hello, you've reached the nut house, Head Cashew speaking. May I help you?"

The response had the boss rolling his eyes.

"Betty Ann, you may *think* E.T.'s going to rip your liver out if you come back to work tomorrow. But I *guarantee* I'll rip your liver out if you don't." With that he hung up, went back to his office, and turned the calls back on.

Yes, it had been the moon. And it had moved slightly. Then Veronica felt something strange, almost physical, happening to her. It reminded her of when she was a kid getting out of a cast and had to rediscover how to use muscles she thought she could no longer command. Or when she was convinced an optical illusion could only be seen one way until it shifted, and she was equally convinced it could only be seen the other way. Gradually, like a sluggish dimmer switch sliding, Veronica began to "see" the tendrils Jason had drawn, twirling slowly, hypnotically, between the Earth and the moon. They began to look like the heads of a woman and her daughter, both with long hair gently intermingling as it blew in an odd breeze between them. *Gravity,* she thought to herself with a huge, excited smile. *I'm actually "seeing" gravity.*

But the next moment her smile was gone when she felt a thought she knew was not her own slither through her. It wasn't in words, but she somehow knew it was the equivalent of: "You've never seen gravity before?"

Panic. Histus hadn't allowed himself to feel it when their enemies cloaked their arrival so effectively that they'd penetrated Mother Planet, killing 75% of the population before the first alarm vibrated. He hadn't allowed himself to feel it when those same enemies found his escape ship, despite his invisible-cloak technology. And he'd firmly avoided feeling it when their enemies attacked again and all those on his ship that did panic perished.

So why did he feel it now? Their enemies must have been deceived when Histus and the few others that didn't panic uploaded themselves into the ship. Why else would they have left them alone for so long? They must have been convinced they had killed everybody aboard which, at least physically, was true and confirmable. The ship itself, with technology so beneath their contempt it wouldn't be worth salvaging, would then be just another uninteresting artifact pointlessly propelling itself around the universe on autopilot.

They were so close now. All they had to do was make it to the center of the galaxy they'd just entered. But Histus felt panic now because he had just discovered a new enemy, an enemy he couldn't possibly escape or deceive: himself.

It had been an endless voyage with far too little to do to keep any of them occupied. Of the few who had survived, most—if not all except himself and Shishum—had long ago gone insane. The best Histus could hope for many was that, once they had new bodies, they would provide breeding stock. And now he was threatening Shishum's tenuous hold on sanity by abusing and threatening his Second in Command?

What was wrong with him? Was it just his having nothing to do? But he already knew.

No one had imagined it would ever be an important issue, but when Histus applied for First in Command the one test he failed, miserably, was enduring sensory deprivation.

Histus directed the same ruthless problem-solving skills that had defined his career on himself. Real thing wasn't available? He had to create the illusion of both purpose and sensory experience.

He gave himself the job of locating where their enemies had landed on his ship by conducting a chemical analysis of the hull. He knew it was make-work, but he could justify it by looking ahead to the day they arrived in their New Mother Planet in the center of this galaxy. If they did recreate their bodies and multiply, the young would want to know the history of their exodus. Histus was researching that story.

He was feeling better already, amusing himself imagining Shishum's shoddy retelling of all they went through to reach a new gas giant that was just right. But he was still fighting how little chemical analysis did for him when changing to the next external sensor pulled him up short.

At first he thought it was a memory of what the view outside the ship had been back when they had bodies so they could interpret the imagery. But it was so vivid that it hit him with what reminded him of physical force. Was this it, the beginning of insanity with him imagining the senses he could no longer stand to be without?

He couldn't help himself; his feelings soared at what felt like his regained sense of weight differentiation. Then the full spectrum of sight unfolded before him. He watched tendrils of gravity swirl and dance between spheres in some planetary system they must have passed through back when they had bodies. Had he actually managed to forget gravity's sweet rhythm? Perceptible even without his sense of vibration? The exquisite grace of its motion? How had he managed to delude himself into thinking sight wasn't the array of senses he missed most?

The star, so much heavier than the refuse caught in orbit around it, its thick tendrils fanning out on all sides to hold the planets that surrounded it. The third planet with its—

And it was gone. Completely. Just as Histus realized with unimaginable yearning that it was not a memory. It had been the planetary system they were currently in.

"Shishum?" he sent, not sure it would even answer.

"His*tum?*"

He was pleased to note that he could ignore being neutered. "Could you tell me which exterior sensor the third hit?"

Shishum told him. It was the one he had just switched to.

"And they are still sending blank messages from that location, where I have a direct communications link?" Histus sent.

"Yes, but I can switch your direct link to the location we sent to."

He wasn't going insane. He could only guess at the mechanics involved but he had been seeing! "No thank you, Shishum. I owe you an apology. There's a reason you're Second in Command and perhaps should be First. Even if some prescience prompted you to do it, what you did was the right choice. At least they're sending."

"Thank you, Histus."

It was back to his masculine name ending. Good sign.

It sent again: "One of the others, Wushum, is sending something to me. It hasn't sent anything to anyone since it...became convinced the rest of us were the enemy uploaded into the ship. I should respond immediately."

Another good sign. "Yes, Shishum. Go."

Alone again, Histus tried to remember what part of the ship this Wushum was, and whether or not it was anything critical that they hadn't been able to work out alternate access to. But then all such thoughts vanished when the current planetary system bloomed before him again.

Vast. Quiet. Beautiful. His feelings were like a whole population waking from their falling slumber to all fly upward as one.

He was concentrating on the dance of gravity between the third and its moon, especially appreciating the aesthetics of the moon's delicate tendrils, when he slowly, eerily, became aware of the other.

Histus knew immediately that this other had been there all the time he had been re-experiencing sight. Subliminally, he'd felt this other's presence the moment it started and absence the moment it stopped. But he'd written it off as some kind of background vibrations from the open-link program. Only now—through a kind of motion, a change—did it give itself away. A telltale swelling of something Histus hadn't realized he was losing until he recognized it in this other: the strength of feeling that could only come from a living entity, not one that had been uploaded into a ship.

But it was alien. Extraordinarily alien. Still he recognized its wonder and delight as they watched the dance of gravity together. For a moment he thought of it, in all its bizarre strangeness, as if it was one of the young in his pouch. And he thought, "You've never seen gravity before?"

He could feel both of them recoiling as he realized it had received his thought. And in its initial panic a wave of its primitive defense options washed over him. Shishum had been right! They only considered fleeing over a solid surface with no thought of flying, let alone swimming. How could his initial assessment as a liquid H_2O planet have been so wrong?

"You…don't see light?" It was the alien asking.

Histus thought this really was like communicating with the young in his pouch. "Nobody can see light, silly. It's invisible."

At first he couldn't understand the thunderous vibrations of the response at all and figured Translate had, not for the first time in its long and tenuous history, failed completely. Then it came, albeit with a considerable delay, just as it all vanished again. He was left, once more, as nothing but some software imbedded in a ship's chemical analysis program with only one sense he kidded himself by referring to as smell.

The thunderous vibrations of its response had been a laugh.

Veronica woke up with dawn lending even the rusty refrigerator out back a sweet peach-tone.

How could anyone not see light?

She still recoiled when she remembered that alien presence in her head but then reflected that it was probably no stranger than the playmates she imagined coming out of the toile wallpaper when she was a kid.

Then she thought again. No. This was a whole lot stranger. For this alien was so remarkably…alien. Veronica had always kept to herself, having learned at an early age that other people were alien, at least to her and her sensibilities, but this was different.

And yet this being had been in her head in a way no fellow human had ever been. If she was lucky enough to live, her prison companions, she strongly suspected, would be far more alien to her than this being.

Speaking of more alien aliens, she heard Margret stir, stumble into the bathroom, flush the toilet, stumble back into her living room/bedroom and, of course, turn on the TV:

"In our top story a statement released by NASA late last night confirms that the SETI 'alien' message was a hoax. SETI originally concluded there was an error in calculating how far away the message came from, but they're now convinced their calculations were accurate about how close the source of the message was. At a NASA press conference a spokesman went on record saying, 'Inside our solar system? If an alien civilization was that close we'd know about it.' He then went on to cite all their recent exploration and the need to support a bill now before Congress which would provide the funding necessary to expand their program beyond the solar system. The spokesman ended by saying, 'This supposedly alien contact must have been a hoax message that someone on Earth bounced around with equipment we've already got deployed in our solar system. But the next one could be the real thing.'"

Veronica then heard them bring up the volume for the actual press conference. When someone brought up the human-interest story about the first graders in Idaho who were convinced that the alien message came from Orion's "fourth star," which they still thought was an alien spacecraft, the NASA spokesman laughed tolerantly. "While we certainly want to encourage all our junior astronomers out there," the spokesman said, "we would like to humbly suggest that not many spacecraft are made of giant, luminous, masses of gas."

However foolish the other adults of her species, it was clear to Veronica that this alien was no imaginary playmate from her childhood.

Was it equally alone?

She was about to head out to the fields to enjoy their vast openness while she still could before going to work. But the next words stopped her cold:

"In other news, CEO Barrington Hamilton, so much in the news of late, has been reported missing. At this time no further information is available. Following up on yesterday's story about the dog that loves to play in lawn sprinklers…"

Veronica walked out the door on her way to the cornfields, her stomach in a knot. What could this mean?

If Barrington meant to frame her in court he would have no reason to discredit himself by disappearing as she had. If he was on his way to Horwedel to kill her, he would want a bogus alibi, establishing his presence elsewhere in case whatever was left of her was ever found. This made no sense.

The only thing she could imagine was that it was for her benefit. Maybe he sought to convince her that he'd stopped looking for her and was saving himself by disappearing like she had. All to give her a false sense of security so she'd stay where she was despite being ID'd on the phone by his friend. And, if he was on his way to Horwedel to murder her, that bogus alibi might be easier to establish retroactively with some cover story about needing a break from the press.

It still didn't feel right somehow. But Veronica knew her limitations and reminded herself that it didn't really matter. The bottom line was she didn't have the resources to flee any farther anyway.

Were these her last moments of freedom?

Heading west, wide-open fields stretched before her.

Was she a fool not to run, even now? Fresh air called her to action. Far off in the distance, lingering night promised to hide her. She was beckoned by every dawn-tinted, urgently waving blade of grass.

But if Barrington had chosen to conceal his whereabouts, the treatment she could expect from this murderer would not be good if he found her alone in this vast green sea. Proving her non-existent guilt would be much easier if he made her disappearance permanent.

If the most she could hope for was life imprisonment rather than death, witnesses could save her. Veronica turned towards the call center. But even the shareholders in the Atlantic Time Zone, in Puerto Rico, weren't awake yet. The call center was still closed and Margret's near blindness would work as much in Barrington's favor as it had in hers.

So she headed for her favorite patch of corn, trailing her fingers through the tall grasses. Like a bee with pollen, she imagined collecting what little remained of the sunrise's sweet light.

What would it be like to have never seen light?

She was happy to see that an ear of corn that had been puny the last time she saw it was catching up with the others. A sudden gust of wind frenzied the shadows of corn stalks dancing across her arms.

The sensuous ballet of light and shadow...

She made a slow 360-degree turn. To the north the corn blocked her view of the call center and the center of town. The wind thrashed at its tops but failed to dislodge an elegant beetle. Constantly readjusting its slender legs to cling to the top of its stalk, it danced a sharply staccato flamenco. With better light its ornately armored back might have been deemed black. But in the slanting new light, at the top of a moving corn stalk, a kaleidoscope of metallic colors glittered across it like a conquistador's silver back plate.

To the east, slivers of early light still shivered off the metal roof of Margret's trailer. Just barely visible, and farther back from the road, Betty Ann's teeny trailer top echoed Margret's. Behind it huge fields of corn stretched on forever toward the still-beautiful daybreak.

What could a sunrise or sunset look like if you couldn't see light?

Far to the south Veronica made out the long dent in the vegetation that marked the interstate. She wondered if the rubber left on the road by her swerving the Rolls into the gas station, and the hitchhiker swerving it out, was still visible. She wondered if the dumpster, where she'd dumped the maid's uniform and the wig mimicking her maid's red hair, had yet been emptied. She wondered if she had it all to do over again, would she do anything differently?

No. She was no criminal mastermind or tech wizard and had had no time to prepare. She had done what she could. Convinced she was a helpless victim, Veronica was about to push aside any further questioning of herself and come to as much peace with the inevitable as she could. But she could feel something pushing at the back of her mind, something that felt like she'd been avoiding it forever.

This could be her last day of freedom, her

last time to stand in these completely open
fields. Veronica wanted to be completely
open and honest with herself. What was that
thought pushing at the back of her mind?

Your whole life is something you did to yourself.

In a heartbeat the full light of day replaced
the soft light of dawn. Usually she turned
away from its harshness, heading for the call
center and hardly looking at anything until she
could lose herself in the postcard from M.
Charbonneau.

You choose, at least at times, not to see light.

*When the writing was all over the walls you chose
not to see what you married because it wasn't pretty.*

*All these years you've pined for M.
Charbonneau, he probably remembers you, if at all, as
a foolish American romantic he bedded easily by crying
on cue.*

Before leaving for work Veronica did
another full, slow turn in the harsh light of
day. Did even the inanimate objects she
imbued with beauty stay beautiful? Or had
hiding in the illusion of the safely permanent
just robbed her of life's fleeting beauty?

The world around her was no longer soft
and misty with the innocence of dawn.

Still, on her way to work she did go back
into Margret's trailer to pick up her other
favorite escapes, her book by Proust and her

childhood scrapbook of beautiful things. And the pale scarf with the Asian temples that she never wore for fear of getting it dirty. Gingerly, she wrapped it around her neck. At least she would have all her treasures with her if she was arrested. Although she had a second reason for bringing her scrapbook, which included a classic old shot of light streaming through the windows of Grand Central Station.

At work Betty Ann got in her way, stretching out cupped hands with something white visible between her fingers.

It no longer mattered if little Betty Ann could ID her. She could call her "Vera"—in that way that showed she knew "Vera" was someone else—all she wanted. Veronica was going to push past. But a new thought stopped her.

Was Betty Ann equally alone?

Betty Ann began to appear like one of her little imaginary playmates from the toile wallpaper of her childhood. Blinking against the vision, she held out her own hands and Betty Ann's violently shaking hands dropped a man's white handkerchief into hers.

It fell open in her hands, revealing a money clip with a few bills.

"We ain't...I mean I ain't no thief," Betty

Ann said stiffly.

Veronica had no idea what she was talking about.

"Oh, and this old piece of junk." Betty Ann fished a ring out of her pocket and dropped it on top. The name written across the band was Cynefrid. "But he…I mean I will do what I have to to protect myself. Now I understand you're going to be very upset, but look at this as a warning so you don't make it necessary for anything like this to happen to…" She trailed off.

Veronica couldn't help herself. She was laughing and crying all at once, overflowing with manically insane relief. Next, a short-lived sorrow, for the Barrington she knew would never have parted with that ring while still alive. That was replaced by thinking she really should be frightened of whoever this "he" was whose identity Betty Ann was protecting. But how could she fear this "he," who may not have saved her from prison but had probably saved her life?

"Your husband…didn't treat you nice?" asked Betty Ann.

"My husband," Veronica answered vehemently, "didn't treat anyone 'nice.'"

"And…your father?"

Veronica looked deeply into her eyes,

trying to understand what Betty Ann could possibly know of her father. Was Betty Ann projecting something about her own father? How horrible might Betty Ann's father have been to make her the way she was? Fathers... Suddenly Veronica shuddered with the realization that her own father hadn't been all that different from Barrington. "Horrible, Betty Ann, just horrible."

"Did you ever read about...did you like JFK?"

Huh? What did JFK have to do with anything? "I adored him! I even read an incomplete manuscript he wrote about a *coup d'état* by Lyndon Johnson."

Betty Ann stopped shaking and smiled.

Veronica still didn't understand what JFK had to do with anything but smiled back. Was this an attempt to befriend her, starting with the discovery of shared interests such as JFK? She assumed the "he" Betty Ann had mentioned by mistake—who must have killed Barrington to get that ring off him—was related to someone Barrington had murdered and knew Barrington did it. Who this was and how he'd gotten in touch with Betty Ann were things Veronica decided it was probably better not to know.

Histus hadn't closed out of the external sensor where he'd re-experienced sight. But even without a body to sense time passing he could calculate that the time he had waited to experience it again was over 200 times longer than the intervals he waited through before. There was the very real—and horrible—possibility that what he was waiting for would not occur again.

"Can you see the light?"

If Histus had had a body, his instinctual defense mechanisms would have had him fly halfway into Mother Planet. But he soon got over being startled and was greatly relieved.

"It's in the long, diagonal lines streaming from Grand Central's arched windows to the floor. Since you can hear my thoughts I thought you might be able to see this picture I have with me. I've been concentrating very hard on it, memorizing every detail."

See light? Despite his previous attempts to calm his nerves by comparing this bizarre creature to one of the young he used to carry in his pouch, he was pretty sure it was an adult. But was it sane? And how would he be able to judge whether it was or not? He wasn't seeing anything but, giving it the benefit of the doubt, Histus furiously adjusted and readjusted the Translate software. He was not surprised to find that this had no effect. Typical Translate!

"Are you even there? I thought I could feel your presence but..."

"I'm here," Histus thought back, "and I'm about to be even more there, since the only thing I haven't tried is deepening the connection between us. Assuming I'm as alien to you as you are to me, I suggest you brace yourself."

Histus had to brace himself. The deeper he went, the weirder it got. It—no, it was beyond strange but he guessed that at least technically it was a she—fueled herself in revolting, criminally immoral ways. Insanely her species' own dead were wasted, there being a taboo against eating them or even feeding them to other species. Instead her species ate all other species. Not only didn't they get permission first, or even wait for them to die, but her species murdered other species.

"But you've always been an excellent First in Command."

Where in Mother Planet was she in his mind that prompted that remark? But before he could find it he finally saw at least a corruption of the picture she'd thought to him about. Diagonal lines extending downwards from arches. But the more he adjusted to this way of "seeing" the more he became convinced that he was seeing multiple images superimposed over each other. Unless…

Again it all vanished. He waited.

When it came back it was clearer, perhaps because she'd been concentrating on the image she described during the interruption. Yes, it was one image if all those superimposed objects weren't objects at all but were visible light. But where would all that light come from at once? The star, of course! He examined the trajectory and realized all the interruptions were because light couldn't pass through solid objects. All the diagonals matched, coming from a single source.

"Your father *was* very proud of you. If those five things I'm seeing in your memory are his 'eyes,' he was always looking at you, not—I assume those are your siblings."

Really? He beaconed in on her location in his memories, and there was his father looking straight at him, steadily despite all the vibrations his siblings were making and his own silence. Histus had forgotten this memory. He'd even forgotten his sibling rivalry, his certainty that his father never noticed him amidst the others.

He discovered that even one who had been reduced to a piece of software could feel joy.

"This is wonderful!" she thought at him. "I can feel your joy! But I've never been this close to anyone, so I'm just discovering how to read and understand it. Is it your memory or my picture that has prompted your joy?"

"Both."

He could feel her wonder, not unlike when she saw gravity for what he gathered was the first time. Again there was that enthusiasm that could only be generated in such delicious excess by something alive. It was contagious.

Then it was gone. He waited.

What came back was another jumble of superimposed images he couldn't make any sense of, especially because it was moving. Finally he realized the star was just barely visible, which helped, but it was still difficult to separate visible light from solid objects. Then it came to him: It wasn't that this method of seeing made it possible to see light, but rather that only light made this method of seeing possible. Even colors weren't uniform, changing when the light changed. These creatures were blind except to light itself, and he wasn't actually seeing anything at all. Still, although he could never accept it as a valid form of sight, he could appreciate its great beauty as an abstract form of art.

"Do you see the colors on the back of the black beetle on the corn stalk?"

"The colors, as in all the other colors, on the object you just indicated is one color?" Histus thought back.

"Yes, from the dawn. I can still remember its beauty. I hope it brings you joy, but I'm sensing a mix—with a lot of analysis I don't quite understand about the differences in how we see."

Using her thoughts as a guide he located the "beetle," moving back and forth on another object, and relaxed into a non-cerebral appreciation of the wonderful colors bouncing off it, doing his best to ignore that they were only an illusionary distortion of the light.

"That's better!" she thought.

He was just beginning to think of this strange, savage creature as one of his young again, when it all vanished again.

In the time before she came back, Histus had the time to be thankful that the third wasn't an H_2O planet after all.

But when she came back with another moving image he realized slowly, and to his horror, that he and Shishum had both been right.

"It's Big Sur. Aren't the cliffs magnificent, and isn't the sunset gorgeous over the Pacific?"

Laughter escaped Veronica as she left the call center for lunch. She was free! She danced in the dust of the street, her squeals of delight destroying the dignity and grace of her classical ballet. Then she squeezed Barrington's ring through her pants pocket, just to be sure she hadn't imagined it. As she made her way to the general store she realized that it wasn't just Barrington's death that had freed her. She looked up at the sky.

Inside the general store she relished the cool and the smell of the old wood as she usually did. But she realized she had never paid the least attention to the proprietor. If she could now find so much like herself in an alien then surely she could find something simpatico in this human.

Veronica peered at the proprietor through a veil of dust that pirouetted within an invading shaft of sunlight. Vaguely she remembered his crinkled fingers giving her change before, but now she concentrated on his face. Its lines mimicked the fine grain in the wood. His deep but mottled tan matched the counter, both worn bare and unevenly colored after decades of use. It was as if the ancient man and the ancient wood were carved from the same tree.

She walked through the veil of dust toward him. He looked up and smiled. Logic told her he had probably smiled every time she'd approached to buy her lunch, but she'd never noticed. Shame flooded her as she, at long last, smiled back.

Veronica could see into the alien's mind, although her heightened awareness told her she wasn't seeing everything. She knew he'd hidden something when she'd shown him that last memory of Big Sur, although she couldn't imagine why. But with the proprietor of the general store she didn't have that advantage so she gazed at him a bit, struggling to somehow see into his mind too.

"Lemme guess," he said with a twinkle in his eye. "You've fallen madly in love with me but you jes' can't work up the courage to tell me so."

Veronica took her cue, looking down at her toes and kicking the dust on the worn floor boards. "You found me out." As the proprietor laughed she watched him stretch his arms out over the back of the counter and was again struck with how at one he seemed with the store. She asked, "Have you worked here long?"

"Sixty-three years."

"Ever have the desire to go elsewhere?" she queried.

"Everythin' I need's right here."

"Which is…?" Veronica asked.

"Lots of sky. Wide open spaces."

"Indeed, I love these things too."

"Also mighty partial to the folks hereabouts," said the proprietor.

"That…I'm learning."

"It's not hard. Just remember to look at what they would like to be, not what they are."

Veronica thought about this as she bought an apple. But she stopped thinking about it when she got outside.

High noon. Not feeling quite as giddy now, Veronica stood still with the dust swirling about her feet in the middle of the deserted street and looked straight up. It was very faint, but she was convinced she was seeing, even then, Orion's "fourth star."

Judging from Margret's TV the media had tired of it and was busy covering the heartwarming story of a teenager who gave up going to her senior prom to be with a dying kitten. A few scientists had commented on a nearby cloud of gas, concerned about its steady approach, but official agencies maintained there was nothing to worry about.

Veronica had spent her whole life ignoring things too. But what was that alien hiding?

What idiots they had been.

They'd always lived deep inside a single planet with no interest in any others, even when their attackers' abandoned ships made exploration possible. The few other planets they knew of were all gas like theirs, all liquid, or all rock—like Shishum had thought this third was. Even travelling as long as they had been, they hadn't previously encountered any planets that were combinations. Perhaps that was only because their enemies had so severely disabled their sensors so early in their voyage that they could manage little more than looking for transmissions. Until the one who'd uploaded into the Converter had gone insane and inaccessible, their H_2O didn't have to start out liquid, and they'd easily found solid H_2O without ever running into anything like this.

Still, it was fairly stupid not to realize that a planet could be a combination of things.

At last Histus was in range. The third had really massive amounts of liquid H_2O. He hated to do it; H_2O was plentiful enough that it shouldn't be hard to locate elsewhere. But they'd just travelled between galaxies with a severely crippled ship and needed liquid H_2O now.

He did feel sorry for the savage who had alleviated his boredom and his sensory deprivation at a time when he so desperately needed both. But it had to be done. He was responsible for the survival of his species. It was hard, but he had to separate himself from a few pretty images.

She had not correctly identified "Eclipse Beats" as a song, and no one else on that liquid-rock planet had either. Shishum had reported they'd had more than enough time, given their communication capacities. So the legal obligations had been satisfied, and the law was fair. Being able to identify music was how they determined mental competency among their own kind. And whose fate was he concerning himself with anyway? The fate of one who, if she had the opportunity, might fuel herself by murdering and devouring him?

It was only when another two-color image appeared, like the first she'd shown him, that he remembered that he hadn't closed out of that external sensor.

"I thought you might be able to appreciate the beauty of our world, to see the way we see more easily, if I showed you a still without so many colors. It's a formal garden in Versailles."

She was right. It was easier for him to "see" this image without the motion and so many colors. And he could appreciate that, as bizarre as the subject matter was, there was a symmetry and a beauty. The more he looked the more it seemed to him that whoever had made that image had spent a lifetime studying their visible light and how to use it to achieve the sublime. A revelation struck him; he was surprised at how desperately he hoped he was right. "The one of your kind who created this image was alive before you had the technology to make images with all the colors you see? Has already been feasted on?"

"Feasted on?"

"Never mind that." Sometimes Translate erred by favoring the literal. "Is already dead?"

"Very sadly, yes."

However illogical, Histus was tremendously relieved to know that he would not bring about the death of the one who had created such an image. But of course he would still be bringing about the death of the one who had showed him that image. Then he felt it. Damn Translate! He'd had to turn the connection between them up too high. That explained both his ability to momentarily feel where she was in his mind, though only because of the strength of her negative reaction, and her ability to get past Hide. But even then she couldn't have gotten past Hide if she hadn't been looking, if she hadn't figured out that he was hiding something. He had underestimated her; there was nothing left to do now but ask: "You know?"

"Yes."

"You realize it's nothing against you? That I do regret having to do that to you?"

"It's not just me."

She flooded him with beauty: Images upon images. Then strange artistic renderings that were made of solid materials. Then vibrations…but it was more. Their equivalent sense translated the differences in how fast things vibrated into something they called pitch. He was astounded by their "music."

"None of the ones of my kind who created these things has yet been feasted on."

Histus could tell that the last part was her consciously choosing to address his way of thinking, not Translate. Suddenly he could feel her diving through myriad pathways in his mind, all at the same time. She was searching, searching. Her force and intensity reminded him of how their enemies had all dived through Mother Planet at once, searching them out, but she was only one. Interlaced with the distinct feeling that she was searching through his entire mind, all at once, was a constant scream of feelings: Panic. Anguish. Desperation. He knew she didn't mean for him to hear those feelings, but amped-up Translate kept repeating them as things like: "No! No! No! This can't happen now that I'm free! Someone I'll never know saved me, so I must save him and all the others I'll never know!"

What had started as a beautiful exchange with her, a sanity-saving sensory input, had turned into an attack. He was barely able to maintain the Hide preventing her from seeing that "Eclipse Beats" was a song. Histus had to close out of that particular external sensor immediately. Soon enough she would be—as all the wasteful, murdering omnivores on her planet would put it—dead.

"Would you throw the young from your pouch if they couldn't pass a competency test designed for adults? Our methods of 'fueling' ourselves may be wrong, but we are more evolved than you are. I wouldn't commit genocide to fuel a ship. I couldn't murder you after exchanging our deepest feelings and sharing so much beauty."

One last "are you sure you want to close your connection with this sensor" prompt and he'd be out. What she was showing him now was his father, another memory he'd forgotten.

"You had just hurt one of your pouch-mates badly and felt very, very sorry. You promised your father that you would never do such a thing again. You promised your father that instead you would always treat *anything alive* as well as he treated you—which was very, very well indeed. You would like to be the son who kept his word to this wonderful father of yours—I can see it—and that's what you are. You have kept your word, and I know you will continue to do so."

He knew she wasn't seeing everything.
He knew he had broken that promise in the
past, and was about to break it again.
Thankfully, their connection had at last closed
out.

Then he heard the final word, not hers
but his—translated into her language because
he must have thought it intensely enough for
Translate to conclude he'd meant it for her.

"Damn."

There was no buzz in Veronica's ear.
There was no shareholder on the line. She
was still in between calls, and the alien was
gone. Not even the depth and vastness she'd
first heard between calls remained.
Something in her bone marrow and her gut,
which had been tying itself into increasingly
tighter knots, told her he would never be
back.

Still, she'd been concentrating so hard she
was sure she'd heard something at the very
end, as faint as a whisper in the wind.
Something that reminded her of a seed taking
tentative root in harsh and hostile ground, but
taking root nonetheless.

To her surprise, she felt her muscles relax. With the connection gone, was it all too easy to hope the whole thing had been a hallucination? Or was it because she had seen that seed of change take root in his mind, even if he hadn't yet seen it?

The boss burst out of his office. "Failing to answer, or hanging up on a call is hereby, officially, grounds for immediate termination."

Veronica didn't look at her postcard. She looked up at the humans she so desperately wanted to save. All of them. After such intense concentration on an alien point of view, they looked monstrous for a moment. Then the wino strained his headset cord to stand. Lost for words for once, he gave her an emphatic thumbs-up while smiling and blinking back tears.

What had he experienced in between calls?

Miss 300 was fixated on her like a guardian angel, apparently not hearing a ringing phone.

Two warm hands caressed Veronica's shoulders. She turned around to find that, after searching so desperately through an alien's mind, she was now able to see what was in Jason's eyes. Explaining sector funds to a shareholder as the boss looked on, Jason could barely reach her with his headset's short cord. Yet even before she remembered his drawings of what gravity looked like, she could see in his eyes that he knew what had just happened. It had been no hallucination.

She shuddered; Jason pulled her to her feet. She saw a comforting steadiness in his eyes—and something else—before he enclosed her in his arms. Then he kissed the top of her head and released her, so he could rip all the alien drawings from his cubicle with a flourish he obviously wanted her to see. He was still explaining sector funds to the shareholder as he tore them in half, dumped them in the garbage, and dusted his hands to indicate it was all done and over. She could see in his glittering eyes that he thought she had accomplished what she had tried so hard to accomplish with that alien. He then ended his call, told Miss 300 he'd be back, and took his usual long strides to vanish out the front door.

Buzz. Veronica looked at her screen.

Barrington's friend again. The automatic dialer must have put him back in the queue because she never got the proxy vote. But she was done being passive.

Barrington must have been murdered by a relative of one of his victims, since that was the only explanation for his having parted with that priceless ring. How Betty Ann got involved with this relative, this "he" she'd mentioned, Veronica didn't know. But Barrington really was missing, dead before he could confirm she was in Kansas.

The man on the phone with her now should be the only person left who could connect her with this place.

She was glad Jason hadn't gotten the call.

She did her best to mimic smacking gum. "Hello. My name is Vera Charbonneau and I'm calling on a recorded line. May I speak to…to…"

"Still having trouble finding my name on some computer screen, Veronica?"

"You. I remember you. The one who calls me Veronica. We got disconnected last time. How ya doin'?"

"You…sounded just like her, still do, and your French is impeccable…but I guess it would be with a last name like Charbonneau."

She smacked her nonexistent gum again and did her best to sound bored. "Yeah, well anyhoo, I'm calling about your investment in…" She got the proxy vote, probably only because he wanted to stay on the phone as long as possible to try to figure out if it was her.

Veronica had been careful not to alter her voice too much, figuring that would be too obvious. At the very least, she was sure she'd made him doubt her identity.

Just as the call ended there was a deafening thud. Her first thought was that Jason had been wrong, and she had accomplished nothing with the alien who had just attacked.

Then she saw that it had been Miss 300 falling to the floor. Blood seeped from her forehead.

Holding a heavy tape dispenser, the boss muttered, "That'll teach you to answer the fucking phone." Heading back to his office, he added, "Betty Ann, get your scrawny ass in here. Now."

Betty Ann ignored him, reaching Miss 300 at the same time Veronica did.

Miss 300 had managed to sit up and was trying to stand. But when she saw Veronica she sat back down to straighten her clothes and hair, apparently unaware of the blood dripping down her forehead. "Don't worry yourself about me, Vera, I'm fine." Her eyes started to roll back.

Veronica and Betty Ann struggled to keep Miss 300 from hitting the floor again, their hands losing their grip on her, their muscles shaking from the strain. Miss 300, struggling to maintain consciousness and to get herself up, lurched against Betty Ann, threatening to topple them both over. But Veronica found Betty Ann's hands beneath Miss 300 and grabbed them, steadying them all. Betty Ann looked into Veronica's eyes.

She realized she could now see into Betty Ann's eyes but, unlike the steadiness in Jason's, Betty Ann's eyes were confusing. Still, though Veronica was new at this, she thought she saw a blaze of blind terror behind Betty Ann's scary look. Was she imagining that the elusive flicker igniting it was guilt? Either way, she was pretty sure that what Betty Ann was afraid of right now was Veronica herself, though Veronica had no idea why. But she smiled reassuringly, giving Betty Ann's hands a comforting squeeze. With a lot of help from Miss 300, they got her to her feet.

Looking over her shoulder, Veronica saw straight into the boss' eyes and stared daggers at him. He shrugged, ogled her chest, and blew her a kiss.

Veronica turned back to Miss 300. "Honey—"

"I'm fine, Vera, don't you worry about me." Miss 300 forced a laugh. "I just had a little accident."

Veronica was able to see the disbelief in Betty Ann's eyes and nod back in agreement. She snatched her treasured, pale scarf from around her neck and gently wiped away the blood on Miss 300's forehead. She was trying to assess the damage but keep Miss 300 from seeing her own blood. "Just fixing your pretty hair," she lied, picking words she thought would resonate with Miss 300. "You know us girls have to stick together. In fact Betty Ann and I were hoping you could authorize a little mental health break after all that spooky stuff between the phone calls, which turned out to be nothing. Could we go over to your pretty trailer right now for…maybe some cheese doodles and girl talk?"

Miss 300 nodded happily.

On their way out the wino held the door open, and Veronica realized she had never really looked at him. All she had seen before was a blur of old age and shabbiness. Now she saw the clarity that animated his blue eyes despite his drunkenness. She kept her tone light, for Miss 300's sake, but riveted the wino with her eyes. "How long you figure us girls will be safe taking some time off in Miss 300's trailer?"

His eyes were deadly serious, though his

light tone matched hers. "From what I know of the boss, I'd say one of you is good for the rest of the day…" He nodded toward Miss 300. "…if the other two of you get back in an hour." He nodded toward Betty Ann and Veronica. Then he nailed Veronica with his eyes and all lightness left his voice. "Ships that pass in the night of space, this ship Earth and those 'harmless gasses' that *will* pass us by. I think we're safe now, that we can be reasonably certain we'll now have 'darkness again and a silence.' You had me worried for a while, as detached as you can be. But you did all right, 'Vera.'"

His Cheshire-cat grin was contagious, but she had to push past him to help catch Miss 300 when she started to swoon again. Partly to keep her conscious, Veronica asked, "Can I ask you a stupid question? Something I should have asked you a very long time ago?"

Miss 300 nodded.

"What's your name?"

"Miss—"

"No, your real name."

Miss 300 looked confused, possibly because she was losing consciousness again.

"Maybe what your mama called you? When she was being nice?"

"Angelina."

"I never knew!" Betty Ann said. "That's a pretty name."

"And you really are an angel," Veronica said softly.

The three women staggered into the sunlight, Veronica feeling the warmth of even Betty Ann's bony extremities as they linked arms to help Angelina steady herself. She saw how the dust swirled about all their feet in the same exact way.

They crossed the railroad tracks and headed for Angelina's pink trailer. Out of habit Veronica started to look off into the distance, at the sparkling fields beyond the town. But she caught herself, bringing her attention back to the two women with her.

Like Ravel's water music, she could see the ebb and flow of a symphony of feelings in their eyes.

Though she had no idea why, Angelina's eyes danced when she thought she had her approval. Maybe Veronica could use that to get her to leave the boss.

Betty Ann darted between acute fear and the swaggering self confidence that Veronica guessed she used to counteract it. Maybe together they could figure out a way to get the boss to leave town and run the call center without him. She hoped she could then figure

Betty Ann out well enough to show her how safe both of them were with most of the people in this town.

Maybe they could all help each other.

Angelina's pink trailer, beckoning up ahead, was no different than Veronica's own retreat into her childhood scrapbook. In their own ways, each sought beauty.

At the end of a very long day, Jason was rattled when he left work for the second time.

Before he left work for the first time, to tell the meadowlark they were all safe, it had been a mistake to embrace Vera/Veronica. It brought back all the feelings he thought he'd left behind, feelings about her that did not include the contempt he'd been clinging to as a defense. But he knew what she'd been through. He had to comfort and reassure her.

He'd experienced the connection with the alien ship's sensor differently than she had—more visually—but he had experienced it. He'd even felt his favorite paleface, the wino, there with them too—though he, like Jason, had been powerless to do anything.

The alien, this Histus, had not heard

either *Jasus* or *the winus*. They could only lurk, unseen and unheard, but they could apparently see what she had accomplished better than she could. Jason had been so overcome that he'd had to run out, at least for a little while, into the prairie she had saved.

Now, to add to the torment, he knew Veronica was behind him, also leaving work. Then he heard her hurried approach before she grabbed his bare arm again.

"Though it'll be quite humble, I'd like to make you dinner," she said.

"I'd...love that."

"Do you mind if it's at your place, not mine? Margret's trailer is—"

"I'd love that too."

Just then they passed Eddie and Ike, staring at the sky. But Eddie stood up slowly at the sight of them arm-in-arm, with a dangerous look on his face that Jason hadn't seen for a long time but recognized all too well from childhood.

Veronica still wasn't letting go of his arm. If anything, she was holding him tighter.

Jason thought about it, affectionately indulging his own prejudices. If a mere woman could take on extraterrestrials... Jason was stronger and faster than the aging Eddie and Ike. He thought about what he'd need to do to immobilize both without putting Veronica at risk. Then he freed his arm from her grasp and wrapped it firmly around her shoulders, staring hard at Eddie.

There was a moment of almost comedic shock on both Eddie and Ike's faces. Then there was a lot of looking at each other expectantly, as if each wanted the other to take Jason on. But they soon went back to staring at the sky. Jason guessed there'd be a lot of that, no matter what the news said, until those "harmless gasses" moved off toward the center of the galaxy.

Veronica snuggled in closer. Jason silently apologized to The Great Graffitied One standing guard in front of the general store for such a deplorable lack of woodenness, and smiled.

A very long time later, Histus was thinking he might be a bit too proud about having a brood of young in the pouch under his wing when another father with his own brood quite literally bumped into Histus' new body. It was then that Histus realized that, when Shishum got its new body, it had not become Shish*a* again but had instead become Shish*us*.

Histus was horrified at the thought of having anything in common with such a fool. Clearly—in this new world at the center of its galaxy—there was little to be proud of in achieving the status of father.

The body collision with this inept idiot of a father threatened to send them all tumbling into the hot core of the New Mother Planet, but even Shishus at last managed to retrieve all his young. When Histus was sure all his own young were not only secure but happy under his wing, he couldn't resist asking, "Did you ever listen to any further transmissions from that third at the edge of the galaxy, the one I stupidly thought was H_2O but you correctly identified as only a rock?"

"Yes," Shishus replied.

Histus immediately regretted asking, recalling all too painfully their time together on the ship. To ask Shishum—Shish*us,* whatever—an open-ended question was to invite an inexhaustible storm of irrelevant chattering. Now that they had bodies again, Histus could see Shishus gearing up for its— his—long-winded answer.

"Something Translate probably didn't get completely right: 'Scientists and religious leaders cringed when an obscure, but brilliant band in New York City, Pioneers of Seduction, cheapened the dignity of the alien transmission by—' You'll love this, Histus: '—declaring it was a song.'" Shishus stopped reading and flashed all his eyes, one at a time for emphasis.

Way too late to have done them any good, thought Histus. He felt the caress of the thin stratum of gasses they were in give way, releasing him to fall, and corrected with a single wing stroke. Idly, he watched the tendrils of gravity tugging Shishus toward the hot core of the New Mother Planet, wondering when, if ever, Shishus would think to correct.

Shishus finally corrected with multiple, clumsy wing strokes. "The band even included their own version of 'Eclipse Beats' in their latest album, calling it 'heavily percussive.' Not a bad version, though it included long segments that were either boringly repetitive or even silent. And I didn't understand their comment about 'heavily percussive.' What other kind of music is there?"

Histus smiled to himself, remembering that now-very-distant planet's melodies, but said nothing.

As Histus had feared, Shishus went on. "That's about it for our song—identified as such long after you told me I was right and there was no H_2O on that planet anyway. Except... Somewhere... Let me scroll...'dog that loves lawn sprinklers goes viral'...no, that's not it..."

Histus was further remembering, not fondly, their time together as first and second in command in the ship that brought its uploaded survivors to their new home. At least, now that he again had a body, he could respond appropriately to Shishus' babbling by getting very, very drowsy.

"'Barrington Hamilton's chauffeur has testified that Mr. Hamilton went to Kansas looking for the wife he was trying to accuse of the murders we now know he committed. The chauffeur went on to say that when the lead on Veronica Hamilton's whereabouts proved false, Mr. Hamilton got the chauffeur out of the way with some excuse about the car needing maintenance so he could stage his own disappearance.' No, that's not it."

Histus was almost asleep.

"Here: 'That obscure but brilliant band, Pioneers of Seduction, was shocked out of their prejudices about Middle America's lack of musical sophistication when a woman in

Kansas, who preferred to remain anonymous, left praise for their latest album on their website.'"

Histus lied about needing to leave for a physical appointment. Still, except for occasional irritants like Shishus, life was good. Histus was aware of the differences between their new home and the one they had lost, but the differences were so minor that many didn't even notice. The current crop of young in his pouch was promising. The youngest, as usual, was unbelievably cute.

Sometimes, though…just every now and then, Histus yearned once again to "see" light.

OTHER BOOKS BY
SUE HOLLISTER BARR

Boomers for the Stars
Craig Healing Springs
Rococo
Twisted

suehollisterbarr.com

www.ingramcontent.com/pod-product-compliance
Lightning Source LLC
Chambersburg PA
CBHW060426130626
46555CB00005B/2238